I0748394

SOULHAUGEN

Whispers from a pile of souls,
guiding humans toward a protopian world.

Arlene Tribo

For my son, Hayden

Front cover image by Nathaniel Regalado

PRINT ISBN: 978-0-6455804-1-9
EBOOK ISBN: 978-0-6455804-2-6

Arlene Tribo is the author of 'Flying Free with my Wonder Soul' published in 2022. She is a mother, a plant-based recipe developer, a strong living proof of transformative personal health and an advocate for human and animal rights protection. She is also one of the leading examples in her community for planetary sustainability. She lives in Melbourne, Australia.

Chapter 1 – Beetroot Juice

7.30am. It's the middle of winter, though Melbourne's sky shines clear and stark. Amelia is all geared up. Safety gloves, goggles, earmuffs, forest green knee-high gumboots, netting over her head, neck, and shoulders.

She put the switch to start. Set the choke to closed. Depressed the safety lever and squeezed the throttle. She opened the choke and allowed the engine to warm up.

Amelia hears the rollicking and churring song of some common Myra. This vegetable garden farm is also home to Khaki Campbell ducks, tiger slugs, snails and translucent worms.

She holds the whipper snipper firmly against the semi-wet ground, pulled the cord three times and the engine starts. She squeezed to release the throttle and opened the choke.

As she stood up, she smells the avobenzone from the sunblock on her face. The pad attached to the harness lies steadily on her muscular thigh. She attached the loop shaft to the spring-loaded hook, holding the whipper snipper steady on the corner of her right hip.

Swinging from left to right, she inhales cold crisp air as she looks towards 100 metres of weeds. She sighs as she sees some persistent rainbow silverbeet.

Within minutes, she's cleared 20 metres while carefully keeping the shape of the no dig beds and clearing the shoulders between them.

For a few seconds she was distracted by an Eastern Grey Kangaroo, who seemed curious and slightly gregarious. After a few seconds of staring, the roo used its tail as an extra leg to propel itself. So, hop she goes. Amelia was concerned that the roo would jump over the garlic beds which were planted mid-fall. She smiled as the roo hopped over each garden bed.

20 metres up ahead, she looks onto what looks like spear thistle. Amelia took this on as an aerobic opportunity and she slashed all the 1.5 metres high weeds in under 12 minutes.

Her ex came to mind. Recalling his last words to her. She tried to block it by counting how many calories she ate yesterday. She counted with her swings, imagining that her swinging movement would make her waistline smaller.

The snipper started to slow down. She knew there is enough petrol in the fuel tank. Then she noticed that the nylon line trimmers have become quite short. She needed to stump the trimmer head on the ground twice which should lengthen the nylon line.

A combination of the smell of petrol, cut weeds and the odour of neutral earthy compost overwhelmed her nose, and she loudly sneezed. As she closed her eyes, she accidentally stumps the snipper too hard on the ground.

Then, a splash of what she thought was juice from beetroot dripped over the netting over her head.

Her instinct knew it doesn't smell like beetroot. She knew she didn't injure her head. And she knew that all the crapaudine beetroot have been harvested four weeks ago. She recalls young farmer Josh getting sore shoulders after digging and harvesting 30 kg of crapaudine beetroot each morning.

Crapaudine beets grow medium to long elongated roots. Carrot-like shape with trailing and overlapping roots. They grow deeper into the ground and have cracked, rough and thick brown skin. Kind of alien looking, really.

Amelia immediately pushed the off button and pulled the red tab at the top of the hook to release the snipper off her thigh and left it on the ground. She quickly stepped and kneeled to investigate where the red liquid is from.

She asked herself, ‘Why does it look like this beetroot has been vacuumed packed?

She turned over the vacuum bag, panicked as she tried to get all the gear off her head to breathe. She saw what seems like remnants of a human hand.

Chapter 2 – Wider World

Jacob: Hi James. Before we start, how much is it an hour again?
James: $25. However, this could be life-changing depending how open you are.
Jacob: Okay. It's just that I just lost my job.
James: It's okay if we go a little bit over an hour. I'm sorry to hear that you lost your job. Though for most people that can be a blessing in disguise.
Jacob: You think?
James: It depends, again to how open you are. We'll make this session quite informal, and I'll just let you speak. I'm here to listen.
Jacob: Well, I'm getting a bit old. I'm turning 28 next month. I umm was working as, umm, a meatworker, in Albert Lea, Minnesota. I was there till they shut it down.
James: What happened?
Jacob: Well, one time, an unannounced inspector came from the feds, umm, not sure what you call them. He was really disgusted about the situation of the pigs. He saw most of them with fractures and open cuts, and the whole place, he said it stunk really bad. It's okay with us but maybe we just got used to it. The weird thing was the pigs seemed to scream louder as soon as they saw the inspector. Especially the sows, the mother pigs.
James: How do you feel about that?
Jacob: At the time, it gave me goosebumps. But now I feel confused. The job gave me money every week but I'm kind of glad that the slaughterhouse is closed.
James: Why do you feel glad about that?
Jacob: Well (sighing slowly and trying to hold back his tears), umm, I feel that the pigs are let free when people from the animal sanctuaries turned up. Hopefully they will have a good life there. Umm, and I'm glad for me too because, even the screeching sound of car tyres reminds me of the screaming and the intense squealing of the pigs. Maybe this smell of 'slaughter' will be gone from my clothes, my hair, and my mind. And, umm, maybe, umm, I would stop having suicidal thoughts.

James: Do you think about just death itself or have you a plan how to die?
Jacob: I really want to stop thinking about it. But I'm thinking of killing myself of how I cut the pigs.
James: Tell me about your loved ones.
Jacob: There's my mom, my brother and little sister. I'm very close to all of them but I cannot support them without a job. My brother lost his job too and he's just been diagnosed with prostate cancer.
James: How would they feel if they lost you?
Jacob: They would be devastated. Lilly my sister would be really sad. That's why I'm here to get help. Umm, I don't what to put a burden on them like my father did.
James: Where is your father?
Jacob: He's gone. He's either in heaven or in limbo.
James: In limbo?
Jacob: Umm, we lost him through suicide. In July 2001, he was doing the same job as I was. But one night, the slaughterhouse burnt down, and he lost his job. After that, he was always drunk. He yelled at me all the time because I wouldn't do my homework.
James: How old were you then?
Jacob: About 6. Maybe, if I had just done my homework maybe he wouldn't have taken his life.
James: I think he decided to exit this world. Most likely, that his mind told him to end the pain he was going through. It had nothing to do with you, Jacob.
Jacob's tears started to flow: I'm sorry, I didn't mean to cry.
James giving Jacob a few minutes: It's good to cry. Now I would like you to repeat after me. I forgive my father.
Jacob: I forgive my father.
James: I forgive myself.
Jacob started hyperventilating while crying: I, umm, I forgive myself.
James: Let it out, Jacob and try to breathe in and out slowly. Take your time.

James was looking at him with great compassion. He sees a 6-year-old boy so lost in his little world.

James: I'm here to listen, okay?

Jacob now starting to calm down: Okay.
James: Every time you have suicidal thoughts. I would like you to say those 2 important sentences.
Jacob: Got it, James.
James starting to smile: What kind of car do you drive?
Jacob: Nissan Pulsar. Why?
James: It's important that you do what I'm about to ask you to do. But firstly, you must answer my question.
Jacob: Do what? What's your question?
James: Do you want to change your life?
Jacob: Yes of course! Look at my life.
James: You rushed the answer. Think about it first. Do you really want to change your life?

Two minutes passed.

Jacob: Yes, yes, I do. It's either suffering and death or, umm, laughter. Yeah man, I would like to laugh again like before dad died. Like, umm, you know, I want to breath freely again.
James: Like a belly laugh that you couldn't stop, and you just lose yourself in the moment?
Jacob showing some light in his eyes: Yeah, man! So, what is it you want me to do?
James: I would like you to spend at least 2 nights and 3 days at the Voyageurs National Park.
Jacob: Oh no, I can't do that. That's almost six hours drive. My car would not make it there.
James: I know. You can borrow my Toyota Hilux so long as you look after it.
Jacob: Oh.
James: You must do it alone.
Jacob: Oh no, I can't be alone. I've never been alone.
James: I promise you will not feel alone there.
Jacob: Oh man, would I sleep in the car?
James: You can but it would be uncomfortable. You can borrow my lightweight solo tent, and I want it back without any damage.
Jacob: You've obviously done this before.
James: Trust me, you will come back feeling a lot better.

70 minutes has passed since Jacob and James met. Jacob exits the door.

James: By the way, Jacob, there's also one thing I would like you to change.
Jacob: What is that?
James: Everything.
Jacob: What do you mean, everything?
James. Change everything. Obviously, not all at once. Every little thing – with the way you breath, the way you look up at the sky, the way you look at yourself, the trees and all the animals. Slowly, one thing at a time.

James threw him the keys and Jacob caught it with his right hand.

James: Got it?
Jacob: Got it.

Jacob woke up at 6am to pack up his drinking water, food, tent, and gear. He stopped by a station to fuel up. As he drove, flashbacks of his childhood run through his head. His dad reading him 'Hairy Maclary from Donaldson's Dairy'. How he used to laugh so hard because his dad would always stutter as he read 'Schnitzel Von Crumm, with a very low tum.' This memory made him smile.

He noticed that it feels good driving James' Hilux. He started to daydream of having one. A few hours passed.

Jacob drove to the primitive camping area of Voyageurs. Hikers and campers without a boat are allowed to park in this area. He was thinking that he can hike-in the campsite along the Kab-Ash trail which extends between the communities of Kabetogama and Ash River.
When he arrived at the camp site, he saw a couple of fire rings. He checked his permit and chose his spot. He walked around and saw that there's enough dead wood to collect for fire.

It's October, the park has a magnificent fall foliage with varying colours and shades. He could feel his heartbeat slowing down. There is no one else there. The fishing and tourist season must be over.

Jacob is feeling hungry by now, so he gathered some wood and set fire on the metal rings. He whistled continuously while he cooked his shore lunch. A Minnesota staple lunch – fried walleye fillets of fish, tartare sauce and crispy fried potatoes. Still sizzling, he started eating his lunch while it blurs his eyeglasses. He just remembered to take out his coleslaw.

When his tummy felt full, he packed up everything including his rubbish. He made sure the fire is completely out. He walked for miles using his map and compass. He could feel his blood flowing through his arms and legs. A brush of pine and conifer scents passed through his ash brown wide nostrils. He hiked 10 kms of the Kab-Ash trail and decided to head back to camp. He was feeling anxious that he might encounter a black bear and cougar.

On the way back, he experienced sights of moose, white-tail deer, fox, beaver, river otter, muskrat, snowshoe hare and weasel. He could hear Canada jays nesting.

He had just enough time to organise his tent before sundown. Jacob set fire in the metal ring again and cooked the same as his shore lunch.

Bedtime. Beside his airbed, he put his knife which he managed to sneak out of the slaughterhouse. He thought, its ready just in case an animal attacked him.

Looking at the knife, he said anxiously: I forgive my father. I forgive myself.

He fell in deep sleep. Some hours later, he heard movements outside his tent. He sat up holding his knife. It felt like a long time to him but perhaps only for 5 minutes. Then, the moving sounds disappeared. He fell asleep while holding the knife. He woke up mid-morning.

Jacob could hear the whisper song of the jays. His round eyes moved from side to side wondering how birds can chirp with melody notes lasting up to one minute. He zipped open his tent and breathe in some fresh air. It's colder than expected but it's nice he thought. 'There's that pine scent again'. He looked up, the sky is stark clear. As he walked around, he noticed that among the fallen dried leaved, there's some decolourisation on one area on the ground. There are patterns of grey and bright red. He went over and saw fur and what seems like blood drippings.

He looked around and quickly grabbed his knife and phone from inside his tent. Then up the hill he saw a grey wolf lying on the ground. He slowly walked toward it, then he realised that the wolf is injured. Somehow, looking straight into the eyes of the wolf, Jacob said, 'It's okay, I will get help. I promise, I will be back. Okay, man?' The wolf slightly lifted its tail. He ran down the hill and grabbed his first aid kit.

It appears that the wolf has open wounds from both back legs. Though they are no longer bleeding. He wrapped gauze over the wounds and gave the wolf lots of water to drink. He tried to call for help with his mobile phone, but the call wouldn't get through. He looked through the eyes of the wolf again and said, "I will get help, and I promise I will be back. Wait for me here, okay, man?" The wolf squints his eyes and slightly raised the tip of his tail.

Jacob run all the way to the visitor centre. He was so short of breath, but he still managed to whisper to himself: *I'm tired of feeling guilty. I've got to save this wolf.*

A ranger at the visitor centre saw him from a distance and ran toward Jacob. Jacob explained the situation and described the location. Ten minutes later, he could hear a helicopter from a distance.
Two hours passed. He was told that Dave will be okay.
Jacob said, "Whose Dave?" The ranger replied, "The wolf you just saved. The conservationist named him King Dave because he is the alpha male in his pack." Jacob could not believe it and he tried to hold back his tears. He was disappointed with himself that he might not see the wolf again. He didn't say anything after that. His father's nickname was Dave.

The ranger hopped into the driver seat to take Jacob back to camp.

Ranger: By the way, I admire the way you handled this whole situation. Most people wouldn't have cared. Would you like to volunteer for a month here and if you like it, you could apply for a job after that? We have a ranger trainee vacancy coming up.

Jacob is just thinking in his head: *No, I can't, I don't have a good car, and I live far away.*

Ranger: Well?

Jacob still thinking in his head, a flashback of James saying the words – *change everything*.

Jacob: Umm, umm, yes, I can do that. I will volunteer and then apply for a job. I love it here.

Chapter 3 – The Flying Warrior

1896, three days after Christmas, Maria Carmen Taimis is daydreaming of singing with her piano again. The head madre told her not to sing love songs at the convento. She wipes her tears off her Española face with her coif. Her cheeks and lips are shaking as she starts to hyperventilate.

Carmen knows what to do to slow her breathing down. She starts humming to herself. She lifts her hands parallel to her elbow as if she's playing the piano. She whispers, "Adios mi amor, te veo en el cielo." She slides her coif off her head. She took off each piece of her habit and put on her white camisa and her long flowing black and yellow wide-stripped saya which covered most of her ankles. Over her shoulders, she put a kerchief cream pañuelo. Around her slim waist, a thin, soft cotton tapis. She felt her hip bones sticking out.

She untangles her long wavy black hair.

She took her key to open her secret box located under the wooden floor. She prepares to inhale opium. Last month, after meeting with a British merchant, she bought enough opium to inhale for the whole day.

She lays in bed, still crying. She sits on the floor, rocking herself, inhaling for hours, deep in thought:

How did I become like this? So stupidly demure, religious, and gentle. I'm supposed to be a warrior helping to free my people. Now it's too late, mi amore, is about to be executed.

Mamita, why could you just not accept that I'm in love with a native? Where did you hide all the letters that he wrote to me?

My, my love, let there be no bullets come out of the gunshots. Te veo en el cielo.

Carmen slowly wore her abaca chinelas. She held onto the rails as she struggled to go down the winding stairs. Her pañuelo fell on the steps and her tapis got caught on the rails.

Carmen fell on the circular terracotta paved ground just outside the garden. She lays flat on her back with her knees slightly bent. Her chinelas came off her right foot. Her left hand on top of her long wavy black her. Her right hand linear to her hip, is holding a brown rosary. The sun reflects over half of her white camisa. She has black circles around her eyes and the middle of her cheeks are pale raw where her tears were continually flowing.

"Cielo", she whispers as she looks directly into the sky. Slowly breathing. Half an hour passed. Then, she took her last breath.

Reincarnation.

2017, Alisa Torres glided her maroon gown as a semi-finalist in the Miss Philippines-New Zealand competition in Auckland. She bows her head as she exits. She is out. Alisa was going through every word she said in her preliminary interview.

The weekend after the competition, she decided to get some fresh air and drove over Tamaki Drive along Mission Bay, heading towards St Heliers. She winds all the windows down. It's humid. She got startled as a police car with a siren hover right behind her. She handed over her driver's license. Inspector Arorangi asked her to get out of her car and took her to the Mission Bay police station.

That same day, she was taken to Wiri, Manukau, at the Auckland women's correction facility. She has been arrested for the use and dealing of methamphetamine.

Inspector Arorangi arranged with the administration staff for a psychologist to see Alisa the next day. Martin Chesney, a psychologist, and a board member of AA Auckland, quickly got to the roots of Alisa's addiction.

She has spent all her 21 years trying to impress her parents. She didn't want to be a doctor. Since she was two, she wanted to be in the performing arts, but her parents discouraged her from becoming an artist.

With good behaviour, Alisa was released from the correction facility after five years.

2022, Alisa decided to move away from her parents and moved back to the Philippines. She managed to get a job as a carer for the elderly in a retirement home for the priests in Leyte. In all her spare time, Alisa practised her freestyle dancing using her own self-expression and improvisation, usually ending in tears.

She often wears her white silky long dress and dances as if she's a butterfly that naturally moves in motion with Jui-jitsu circles. She dances with her breathing. She times her movements with the silent low waves from the water of Lake Bito. She could not hear her steps as her feet smoothly glides inside the pure black sand around the lake.

She planned to wake up at 4.00am the next day to go back to the lake. She put her camera and tripod beside her bedroom door. She daydreams her video recording will capture her dancing in her white dress over the black sand during dawn. With the help of moonlight, she hopes this would make her look like she's flying.

She arrives with her bare feet rubbing against the sand. She's surprised. She thought she would be alone there. She finds a group of men driving trucks and diggers. She stares at a machinery she has never seen before. It's sucking up the sand.

Chapter 4 – I Will Find You

1803, Thomas James, a young lad of 23, was wandering at a local market in London. A stunning costermonger looked him directly in his eyes, with her sweet voice, she asked him to take a wheelbarrow of fruits and vegetables to a nearby plethora of eateries. Ten metres before he arrived there, he was approached by a bobby, and he was falsely arrested for theft.

Thomas was put into Sydney Cove, a ship which transported convicts to New South Wales, Australia. With the other convicts onboard, they were shifted to another ship to go to an enclosed settlement in Sullivan Bay, Melbourne.

After months of limited water, Thomas and his friends planned to escape. On Christmas eve, while the guards were heavily drunk, they stole a kettle, boots, guns, and medical supplies.

They walked by foot and ate bush food and shellfish. After a few days, Thomas' friends became afraid of the aboriginal people and headed back to the settlement. Thomas said to them, "I rather suffer in the bush, than forego of my freedom." So, he carried on walking until he arrived at Port Philip Bay.

After a month of isolation, he managed to befriend a couple of aboriginal people, and they taught him how to fish. A decade later, he assimilated with the Wallarranga tribe and fluently spoke their language. He laughed, dressed, and hunted like them. He later fell in love with Murmin, one of the aboriginal young women in the tribe who later became his wife.

Another decade has passed, the British colony has significantly grown, and Thomas was asked by a ship captain to be a translator between the tribe and the Brits. Five days after that, Thomas changed his hunting clothes to a black suit and white shirt. It reflected and matched his jet-black hair, beard and eyes. Within a month, he left the tribe and left his wife.

Eight years passed; Thomas is often seen alone staring at the horizon. He never told anyone that he is illiterate and that he doesn't know where he belongs. He was often heard whispering the words:

"Murmin, rianna, puggalena parnock boorack, rianna riacunha." [1]

"Murmin, dance, like sunrise, dance."

Reincarnation.

1993, California State University graduate, Christopher Johnson, was asked to study the Yanomami's protein intake in the northernmost part of the Amazon.

Chris did a thorough study of the Yanomami tribe for 12 months. He went back home and carefully put together his presentation. He was ready to amaze the panel of professors and important affluent sponsors.

He buttons up his black suit over his white shirt and said, "Ladies and Gentlemen, please allow me to first of all, show you some of my photographs of the amazing Yanomami community."

The first photograph that appeared is that of a Yanomami woman, Marima.

Chris paused. He is lost for words. After about 10 seconds, he said, "I'm sorry, I cannot do this." He left the stage.

Chris spent the next 2 years with the Yanomami tribe. He fell in love with Marima and took her back to California.

Chris and Marima had a son, and they named him Michael. The family lived happily until Michael's 7th birthday. Marima decided to go back and reconnect with her tribe.

Michael cried for months, longing for his mother. He repeatedly wrote a letter to her and gave them to his father. He wrote:

Dear Mommy,

Please come back home. The kids at school are always making fun of me. They are saying nasty things about you. I promise, I will find you. I will study really hard, and then, I will find and see you again. [2]

Love,
Michael

Chapter 5 – Intense Ocean

1976, Magdalena Molina is asking her abuelo (grandfather), Pablo, to take her for a swim. Magdalena swims level on the water. Her strokes are long and smooth, and she's only five. Her and abuelo swim almost every day.

Pablo tells his stories to Magdalena at bedtime. Before he says good night and kiss her forehead, His last sentence to her is always:

"Que dios te permita ser el mejor nadador del mundo."
(May god let you be the best swimmer in the world.)

Pablo's parents are originally from the Limon province of Costa Rica. They are members of the Bribri tribe who grew and harvested cacao. Pablo's parents adventurous spirit led them to migrate to the Northwestern part of the country, in Guanacaste, with endless beaches and calm water popular for diving.

Three generation of Pablo's family live in Guanacaste, only a few steps from Laguna del Arenal (Lake Arenal). They grow their own fruits and vegetable in their naturally rich volcanic soil.

Pablo, though short, is masculado. He is known as the best swimmer and diver in Playa Blanca. He stands out like a sore thumb as he socialises and laughs out load with his mestiza and mestizo friends. Pablo's deep brown, red-toned skin contrasts the white gravel and white-washed colonial houses.

The community calls on Pablo whenever there is someone in trouble in the water. He has saved many from drowning.

One hot weekend over Easter in 1985, the town alcalde's (mayor) daughter was swept away by the current. Pablo got to her. He did his best to diagonally swim to the shore. The 12-year-old girl had breathed in too much water, and it was too late, despite the ambulance officers and the locals' efforts to revive her.

After a few months, resentment from the alcalde's family grew towards Pablo. Pablo decided to not react and just ignored them.

Magdalena, only at 14, gave her Abuela the idea of building a swimming and diving school at Playa Blanca. In just five years, the abuelo and la hija grande duo had grown the school to the biggest one in Costa Rica.

The Molina family consistently made profits from the school. The family sent Magdalena to study marine biology at the University of Liverpool. She got tired of the cold in the UK, so she proceeded to study her master's at the James Cook University in Queensland, Australia. To be closer to home, she did her PhD at the University of Florida.

Over the last 12 years, abuelo and Magdalena stayed connected over the phone and through writing letters to each other. Both excited, checking their mailbox, exchanging stories about sea creatures.

Magdalena worked part-time throughout her studies, while the Molina family kept up with growing their school all over Costa Rica.

Magdalena decided to come back home and had been offered a job in the government under the UNCLOS (United Nations Convention on the Law of the Sea).

Magdalena is paid well at her job, so she took abuelo overseas, even now at the age of 81, he is still very energetic. They went diving at Julian Rocks, Byron Bay, Sydney, Australia.

Upon returning home around sunrise, while the plane is landing, she noticed about 100 kilometres of fishing line. An industrial fishing is happening right before her eyes.

Magdalena and abuelo did their best to get to the fishing site. Turtles, dolphins, mahimahi, stingrays, yellowfin tuna and silky sharks are trapped in the fishing line and they're already dead.

Despite Magdalena's efforts at work to avoid incidences like this, she was feeling hopeless. She later found out that some money was being exchanged between the local government and the bosses of the fishing industry.

Magdalena knows in her heart, that in just two and a half decades, the diversity life in the Costa Rican Ocean has decreased significantly.

Frustrated, she had a sleepless night. She still woke up early to make abuelo's casado plate: gallo pinto (savoury and spicy rice and red beans), hearts of palm ceviche, fried green plantains, chillero hot sauce, nixtamal tortillas and fresh half avocado.

While she's cooking, the home phone rang. She answers, "Hola." On the other side of the phone line is the head of Mission Blue, explaining to her that they are looking for a marine conservation champion in Costa Rica, and if she would be interested in applying.

Chapter 6 – Which World is Home?

It's summer in mid-June, Martin Vordr is driving along the Atlantic Ocean Road which connect the town of Molde, passing through the island of Kristiansund, Norway.

The high tide wet the road. Martin was speeding through the corner. He didn't want to be late to his date. He lost control of his car, and it landed on the water. Martin drowned and died, at the age of 26.

Martin's soul has 40 days to say goodbye to his loved ones.

On day 38, he went back to his family church, an Evangelical Lutheran church. Toward the end of his prayers, he is feeling very resentful, to a point that he is feeling angry. He walked the middle isle, leaving the church, he screams, "Why? I've been good all my life. Why, why do you have to end my life so soon?"

He run as fast as he could, noticing his body is become more like the colour of fire. White fire-like as if his legs are burning wood inside a fireplace. He could not believe that he is not getting tired. He must have been running for at least a day. His soul knew he's been running for over 9,000 kms.

Then, on the corner of his eye, he thought he saw a giant white butterfly. He slowed down and did a sharp turn to find out what it is.

He stared at it. Without blinking, he questions himself: *Is that an angel?* On the back of his mind, he is telling himself: *No, I'm not ready to go.* He wanted to run again but he didn't. He started watching the giant butterfly. He felt hypnotised. As he fights himself from getting any deeper, he realised that the butterfly is a girl dressed in white.

He is thinking though, that angels mentioned in the Bible are masculine men who serve as messengers of God.

Today is day 40. There's a set of fire-like lights hovering behind him from a distance. He run closer to the girl. He thought, that if she's not an angel, then she must be just a pagan.

He moved as far away from the set of lights and watched the girl dance in her white dress. It's Alisa Torres. He noticed himself smiling again.

Determined not to go to another world, he followed her home, watched her get her camera and equipment ready for the next morning. He watched her sleep.

Chapter 7 – Uncontrollable

Sean went down on his knees to reach for the parking ticket which the wind blew off under his car after he took it from the windscreen wiper.

His car is parked along the Auckland District Court in Albert Street. "Blast, 28 bucks!" He said. "Well at least that's still cheaper than Wilson parking."

Sean walked a few metres south to meet with Peter at the Kingston Street Café. They started going through the brief of evidence for tomorrow's deposition.

It's 12.30am. Sean is still preparing the documents. Sitting on his office chair at home in Mt Eden, he's using a highlighter which he got from the $2 shop. It started to sting his eyes. The colour of the yellow highlighter turned kaki brown on the pages.

He peeked through his white wooden plantation blinds. It's full moon tonight. He went to bed, but he couldn't sleep.

It's 3am. He Googled 'How to reverse pre-diabetes.' He stumbled upon a challenge called 7-7-7. A challenge of 7 marathons in 7 days in 7 continents. His eyes lit up with excitement. He chuckled to himself thinking he is crazy enough to even think he can to this. He loved running in high school. It would be a great way to shed his excess weight. It would force him to eat better and train running for a few months. He wondered if it would make his blood test results go back to normal.

He clicked on the FAQs tab. Selected schedule and cost.

Big sigh, he sat back and hugged one of his pillows. EUR 30,900. Converted to NZD 72,170.

He peeked through the upper part of his shutters and said, "Mr Moon, what do you think? Should I do this crazy challenge? I could sell some of my shares. I have high-profile cases I should collect big fees from. I will train hard, and I have a year to prepare for this. Well, Mr Moon, what do you think?"

Sean went to his garage. He took one of his shoes and put it beside his bed where his feet lands as soon as he gets up.

Seans smiled slightly and said, "I'll take that as a yes."

Though Sean only slept for 2 hours, he went for a 30-minute slow run in the morning. He felt energised and his deposition with his client went well.

He went to Huckleberry to get some organic food. Sean had lunch at home and worked in his home office for the rest of the day.

He registered for the challenge and smiled as he read that he could pay for the fees in three instalments.

He grabbed an A3 printing paper and stuck it on the wall. He put a giant upper case letter T on it.

On top of the left-hand side of the T, he wrote 'CONTROLLABLES'. On the top right-hand side, he wrote 'UNCONTROLLABLES'.

In the CONTROLLABLES side he wrote:

1. Run 5 days a week, incrementally add at least half a km each time.
2. Delete Uber Eats app from my phone and schedule a weekly home delivery from Huckleberry.
3. When I get the confirmation that I'm in the challenge, call ABN AMRO Craigs to partially withdraw my shares.

Sean stared at the UNCONTROLLABLE side of the page for a while. He couldn't come up with anything to write, so he left it blank for now.

He was thinking that he hasn't felt this good since high school.

Saturday night. Sean is pleased with himself because he's run for 5 days during the week, and he can run 5kms non-stop.

He checked his email. The good news arrived. He's been accepted in the challenge.

Sean was jumping for joy like a child. He called his assistant Peter to relay the good news. Sean's immediate thought is to celebrate with pizza and beer.

He didn't tell Peter that he instead cooked portobello with creamy cashew sauce, thyme, garlic, and artichoke hearts. He also made puttanesca spaghetti and a large cheese and onion salad.

Sean rang Peter to ask him to scoot over at Liquorland to get some non-alcoholic Heineken.

Chapter 8 – Journal Whispers

Yoshinori Andrews is a chef in Sydney, Australia. Nicknamed Yoshi, he is a tall, handsome 44-year-old mix of Australian, Chinese and Japanese.

Despite his good looks, he is single by choice and wants to be close to his family. He lives with his grandfather, Kiyoshi and his parents, Brett, and Olivia.

Yoshi came home late. Even though he tried to be quiet, he found his grandpa awoken up by his footsteps. They chatted briefly in the kitchen. Kiyoshi is half-Japanese, half-Chinese. He was explaining to Yoshi that in 1937, when he was 4, his family moved to Australia. That when his parents forgot to take their 'badge' to the community leader, they weren't allowed to be given any rice.

Kiyoshi said that by 1953, when he just turned 20, he was helping his parents run their Chinese restaurant.

Kiyoshi said "You know, the uncultured drunks used to come to our restaurant after the pubs closed. They made so much trouble. They didn't like the Chinese, but they keep eating Chinese food". He chuckles. He then said, "Even though they were loud and messy, they always paid for their food."

The restaurant has been passed on to Brett and Olivia and now to Yoshi.

Yoshi trained to become a chef in his 20s. By the time he turned 35, he became a Certified Professional chef.

Two years ago, Yoshi's restaurant which he renamed 'Mr Hong' won a Michelin star.

Since then, Yoshi started planning to build another restaurant. Though the plan has been put on hold. His father Brett, who is one of the main cooks, has been sick lately. He was recently diagnosed with high-blood pressure and arthritis. He has been in chronic pain lately and can only work up to three hours a day. Two months later, Yoshi's mother was diagnosed with type-2 diabetes.

Yoshi was asking his parents, "How come grandpa is healthy and fit as a fiddle?" His parents look at him with a blank face and said, "I don't know!"

That night, Yoshi took out his journal. He started writing and asking questions. He wrote that the difference between his grandpa and his parents is that his grandpa occasionally ate, meat, dairy and eggs. When he does, it's so miniscule that it is more like a treat.

On Yoshi's day off, after going to the Orange Grove Farmers Market, he slowly marched to his local library. He came across 'The Cheese Trap' [3] by Dr Neal Barnard. He borrowed it along with a book about the history of Japan.

That night, he learned from 'The Cheese Trap' how dairy cheese could lead to health problems and that dairy cheese contains opiates that make cheese addictive, triggering the same brain receptors as heroin and morphine.

Yoshi thought to himself: *What the hell?*

From the book of history of Japan, he learned that the country, by royal decree, was a vegan country for 800 years. He learned that temple monks have been practicing vegan food for centuries.

During the Christmas break, he took two weeks off to go to Japan and Korea to study Buddhist and temple food.

He learned how to make vegan pound cake made with okura, which is a by-product of tofu making. It's that part of soybean which is high in fibre.

He learned how to make a mock-up turkey meat using seitan. The seitan is then wrapped with a skin-like product made of yuba, imitating the skin of the turkey.

He knew that his parents ate a lot of cheese every day, so he made it a mission to learn how to make vegan cheese while in Japan.

Yoshi knew that dairy cheese is both fermented and coagulated. He was writing in his journal that tofu is coagulated but it's mostly not fermented. He's heard of fermented tofu products such as tempeh and natto, though they don't give that gooey texture and cheesy smell.

Yoshi came home feeling his trip was half-accomplished.

While opening the doors of Mr Hong, a young man turned up. The young man said, "Hi, I'm Alan Wigmore, I spoke to you on the phone last week." Yoshi replied: "Ah, yeah, you're our new dishy while Lochie is on holiday. Nice to meet you, mate. Come in, I'll show you around."

After two weeks, Lochie rang Yoshi to say that he is staying in Italy for a while. Luckily, Alan can stay for a few months and is happy to keep working at Mr Hong.

One night, Yoshi stayed behind at the restaurant trying to mimic dairy cheese with all kinds of ingredients. He was getting frustrated as none of his creations came remotely close to looking or tasting like cheese.

Alan, while still doing the last batch of the dishes: What exactly are your making, man?
Yoshi: I'm trying to make vegan cheese. First, I need to make it smell like cheese.
Alan: I remember my grandma used to make rejuvelac that smells exactly like cheese.
Yoshi: What is rejuvelac?
Alan: She used to soak grains on water inside a jar, she washed and rinsed them and soak them again for a few days.
Yoshi: What kind of grains did she used?

Alan: I don't know, sorry. She's originally from Lithuania so she liked her grains and herbs and stuff like that.
Yoshi: Okay, let's Google it, what grains did Lithuanians eat? in, say, 1920?

The next day, Yoshi bought some millet and buckwheat. He washed, rinsed, and soak them for a few days. He noticed that the water is getting cloudy. The result is that it started to smell funky. So, he threw them away.

Yoshi is wondering: *Okay, what grains do we have here in the kitchen, ah, rice and quinoa. Let's see if this will work.*

After a week of washing, rinsing, and soaking:

Yoshi: Yes, it smells a bit cheesy. Or maybe I'm just getting obsessed. Here, can you have a smell, Alan?
Alan: Yeah man, that smells a little like cheese.
Yoshi: Yeah, I though it's quite weak, but I think I'm getting closer, eh?

Yoshi then soaked the rice and quinoa for two more days.
Yoshi disappointingly nodding: Blast! It's smells like vinegar!

Alan shakes his head as he watched Yoshi threw away the rejuvelac. Alan is also smiling because he knows his boss is not about to give up.

Yoshi is writing in his journal before he went to bed: *There must be some elements in rice and quinoa that makes it smells like cheese. Okay, what would reduce the elements of this good stuff. Hmm, okay, maybe while the rice and quinoa are grown, the good stuff is reduced by pesticides.*

Yoshi dropped by the nearest organic shop on his day off and bought some organic rice and quinoa.

A week later. "Eurika!", Yoshi yelled. Alan dropped a plate and smashed it on the floor. "Man, you scared the shit out of me. What happened?"

“I got it, man, I got it!” Yoshi speaks with loud excitement. He continued, “Here, smell this.”

Alan said, “Ah! It smells like old socks, Yoshi.” Yoshi gently nudged the side of Alan’s head. Alan said, “Just kidding, man, you nailed it, Yoshi, that smells like some real mother fucking cheese.”

Alan and Yoshi finished up the cleaning while listening to ‘Seven Army Nation.’

On Yoshi’s day off, while the restaurant is closed. He is trying to semi-solidify his cheese. He tried to use a dehydrator, but they were cracking.

Every week for nine months, Yoshi reiterated different types of vegan cheese with different combinations of grains and seeds. He now has four different cheese varieties, one that is reminiscent of camembert, one that is smoked, one like mozzarella and one like haloumi.

When he got home, he would gradually replace the dairy cheese with his cheese creations in the fridge. He never told his parents that they were plant-based. One time, Yoshi’s mum, Olivia, told him that these cheeses are “A little different but they’re so yummy”.

Five months later, Brett’s blood pressure has significantly improved and the joints in his hands and feet are a lot less swollen. Olivia just pulled up at the driveway, both Brett and Yoshi came out to greet her with a kiss. Olivia said, “I just came back from my doctor, and she said that my blood results are back to normal. So, she is gradually reducing my medications.”

Not long after that, Yoshi decided to change half of Mr Hong’s menu to plant-based. He carefully incorporated Buddhist temple food and his cheese creations.

After two months, only 12 people ordered the plant-based dishes. Another, three months had passed, and word of mouth spread that his plant-based dishes are so delectable.

One of the customers asked for the head chef after eating his vegan meal. The customer was praising the cheese and explained to Yoshi how it blended so well with the dish.

Yoshi explained to him the story of how his parents like eating his cheese creations and that it seemed to have reversed their high-blood pressure, arthritis, and type-2 diabetes.

Two weeks later, Yoshi got a call from the NSW Food Australia Complaints Commission (FACC).

The customer he was speaking to praising his cheese happened to be a food critic and wrote an article about Mr Hong in the Sydney Times.

After two hours of investigation at Mr Hong, NSW FACC suspended the restaurant's trading until further notice. He was accused of making false claims that his cheese provided health benefits.

Yoshi reassured his staff that he will do his best to have Mr Hong up and running in no time.

As Yoshi locks the back door, a middle-aged heavily bearded man was sneering at Yoshi and said, "You Asians should stop doing dodgy things." Yoshi just shook his head and replied to the bearded man, "Anyone can be dodgy. You need to be smart enough to see who the real dodgy people are in this world."

He came home, went straight to his bedroom, writing in his journal once again.

The next day, he opened his journal, reading out loud what he had written, and practiced every sentence he wanted to say.

Chapter 9 – Calm Acceptance

The police arrived 45 minutes later. Inside the big 3-walled farm shed, Amelia's hands and knees are shaking while she is being comforted by the other farmers.

The 20-acre vegetable farm had to close for two weekdays while investigations took place. Amelia spent a couple of hours at the local police station to make her statements.

Amelia rang her mum, Kathrin, to explain what had happened. Her mum said that she and her partner Stephan, are visiting Rudolph, Amelia's great grandfather, in Moreton Bay, Brisbane, for a long weekend. Kathrin, with her calm and warm voice, told Amelia that she is welcome to stay at their home, though Kathrin thinks that it's not a good idea for Amelia to stay there alone. So, Kathrin invited her to go with them to Moreton Bay. Though Amelia hesitated a couple of times, Kathryn convinced her to join them.

Amelia's great grandfather, Rudolph Steinbach is 94 years old.

Over the last five years, since Amelia turned 18, she avoided Rudolph, nicknamed Rudy. Both are very articulate about their opinions. They often disagree about many things. Their first argument was over the fact that Rudy told Amelia off for being friends with coloured teenagers.

When Rudy was about 9 years old, he was playing outside with his little brother. While admiring an aircraft up in the sky, he squinted his eyes, and he saw two black dots. Moments later, his surroundings turned into dust and bricks were flying everywhere. Beside a mild injury on his shoulder, both Rudy and his brother were fine. That was the first of September 1939. When Germany invaded Poland.

Rudy's parents immigrated from Germany to Selesia, Poland. Rudy's family were considered as Ruckgedeutschete. Persons of German descent who has been assimilated into the Polish culture but can be 're-Germanised'.

Rudy, as a father, grandfather, and great grandfather, had always emphasised, while telling his WWII stories, that he had a good life during the war. Rudy's parents had joined the Nazi party because it was safer for the family and easier for them to get a job in the surrounding wineries.

Kathryn rung Rudy to ask him to be gentler with Amelia when they arrive at his place.

At the front door, Rudy gave Amelia a big hug and said, "It's so good to see you again." Amelia quietly said "Oh, thank you."

During dinner, Amelia avoided the bread and potatoes. She ate mainly schnitzel, sausages and vegetables. While eating, she was counting the calories in her head. After the main meal, the family had Harzer. A German cheese made from cow's milk. It has a strong and pungent aroma and flavoured with caraway. It's a cheese log smeared with red bacteria, which makes it spicier than the yellow one. Rudy bought it because he knows that it's Amelia's favourite.

Saturday morning, it's Australia's referendum to change the constitution to give the Aboriginal people a voice. The family started to discuss their votes. Rudy closed the car door and said, "Well, can I presume we all voted - No?" Kathryn and Stephan said, "Of course." Amelia just nodded ''Yup." Even though she voted – Yes.

Amelia is quite happy with her reconnection with Rudy. She seems to have accepted their differences.

Sunday night, at the dinner table, Amelia mentioned that she would like to volunteer and go WWOOFing (Worldwide Opportunities on Organic Farms). She was planning to do that at the Krishna Village in NSW (New South Wales) for a month. She hasn't book because she said it will take her a while to save up. Rudy said, "Don't worry about it, Amelia, I'll cover you" Amelia, with her surprised big green eyes, said "Are you sure, Opa?" Rudy answered, "Consider it as your birthday present for the last five years."

Laughter surrounds the four walls of Rudy's home. Amelia paused every now and then, just staring at Rudy's paintings on the dining room wall. In the back of her mind, she's telling herself she should be ringing her friends who are part Aboriginal, as they would be both sad and disappointed about the referendum result.

For dessert, Kathrin made Rote Grautze (red fruit pudding). She made it the traditional way with shiraz grapes, cinnamon bark, a few slices of lemon. She simmered the mixture in very low heat for 10 minutes and let it sit for a while, so the red colour comes of the of grape skin. She strained it through a sieve to get most of the juice. She added some water and sugar to the juice. Then she sprinkled some sago in the juice and left it in the fridge overnight. The next day, she cooked it in low heat, keeping cooking time to a minimum so it retains its beautiful red colour. Once cooled down, she put the pudding in 4 glass tumblers to chill. After dinner, she served them with runny cream on top.

Early Monday morning, the family hug each other at the front door. As Kathrin, Stephan and Amelia wave their hands to say "Bye", Rudy stands tall on his lawn, still lean and strong.

Amelia seems fine working back at the farm. Though she's been assigned more in the kitchen to cook morning tea and lunch.

Her manager approved her leave so she can stay at the Krishna yoga retreat and WWOOF centre. On her first night there, she made a note on her phone that hopefully this place will make her think clearly. She hopes that before the end of her stay, she would have her options about her near future written down.

Amelia was smiling throughout her first half day at the retreat centre. Her and the other volunteers filled 120 slim sacks with mixed sand and gravel. They pulled, carried and slid heavy tarps across to cover the no dig beds at lines 5, 6 and 7. They then put the heavy sacks at the ends and corners of the tarps in keep the tarps secure. They propagated horseradish into lines 8 and 9. They transplanted salad varieties in lines 10, 11 and 12.

By mid-afternoon, they gathered outside on the large deck to do yoga and meditation. Amelia had her eyes closed for a while. She felt a gaze perception. She tried to ignore it and she focused back to her centre.

Amelia felt peace while meditating. Then, she turned her head to her left, she slowly opened her eyes. A guy, perhaps two years older than her, was looking at her and smiled. Quietly, he whispered with his Californian accent, “Hi, I’m Michael.”

Chapter 10 – Good Intention Leads to Another

Jacob rang James to tell him what had happened at the Voyageurs National Park. James said he is so happy for him. James advised Jacob to stay at the park, and he will just pick up the Hi-Lux, gear, and tent next weekend.

The ranger rang Jacob's old employer for reference. The ranger is happy for Jacob to stay in one of the Park's lodges for a month while he volunteers. Jacob had a quick shower. In his small bedroom, Jacob sits on the edge of his single bed, thinking, how amazed he is, how his life turned around in just a few days. How he was worried that things could only get worst after he lost his job, and somehow it actually got better.

Jacob rang his mother and calmly told her that they would have to be behind on paying their bills for six weeks, just until he gets his first pay from the park.

Three months had passed; it's now almost end of January. Jacob kept in touch with his psychologist, James.

James recommended to Jacob that though he is now a permanent employee at the park; to start thinking about studying part time so he becomes a qualified ranger. James also mentioned that Jacob could help his brother out by asking the ranger if his brother could volunteer there.

Jacob learned so much working at the National Park. He also started to save some of his earnings because he is staying rent free at the lodge. He is feeling a little empty inside though. He's been waiting to see King Dave again. The head ranger reiterated that Dave recovered well and that he is back leading his pack.

It's bedtime. It's -21 degrees Celsius. Jacob is thinking he should be used to the cold by now. He started dreaming about going for a holiday somewhere warm. He was wondering how much personal loan he could borrow from his bank. He Googled Skyscanner for cheap airfares. He found a location. He logged in to his Wells Fargo Bank app to get a quote for personal loan.

The next day, he asked the head ranger if he could take a two-day annual leave and explained he is planning to take a 4-day long weekend trip somewhere warm. The ranger explained, "Let me see first from the others who might be available while you are off those days. Give me two days and I will let you know."

Approved. Both his annual leave and his personal loan. Jacob took James' advise to keep his loan to a minimum. Jacob booked his flight and got a small room with Airbnb.

Jacob packed his carry-on bag. That's all he's taking. He woke up during dawn. He turned toward the carpark. He stepped backward as he saw two gleaming eyes in the dark. He paused and stood still. Then, he realised, it's King Dave. They stared at each other for a moment. Jacob thought that Dave must have been watching over him since. Jacob then said, "It's okay, Dave. I promise I will be back." Jacob's pick up arrived, and he proceeded to the airport.

Jacob is gleaming under the bright sun. He joked to himself that he feels like he's literally defrosting. That he's not worried about getting dark as he is already black. He took off his shirt and only now he suddenly realised that his body has become quite lean since he started working at the park.

As Jacob ran toward the ocean, he heard a woman saying, "Excuse me, sir. Sir, could you help me, please?" He noticed the woman's voice had a hybridised accent. Jacob turned and nervously paused as he sees a naturally beautiful woman in front of him. He said, "Sure, what can I help you with?" The woman said, "There's a leatherback turtle ashore and he's too heavy for me. I'm trying to put him back in the ocean."

They ran to the turtle and Jacob said to the turtle, “Hey, buddy. You must be at least 2 metres long and about 800 pounds?” They gently carried Mr Turtle back to the ocean.

The woman sighed with relief and said, “Thank you.” She extended her hand to Jacob and said, “By the way, my name is Magdalena. I work for Mission Blue.” Jacob shook her hand and said, “What an awesome job you have.” Magdalena said, “What brings you here in Osa Peninsula in Costa Rica?”

They chatted for 10 minutes and instantly made a connection about their love for nature. Magdalena turned around and said, “Well, I hope you enjoy the rest of your stay here. Bye!” Jacob watched her back till she disappeared.

Chapter 11 – Why is the Answer

Sean is listening to the race director's briefing in Cape Town. He sees his shadow on the laminated vinyl floor. He can't believe how much weight he's shed in the last year. His running has given him a new force of energy. He somehow feels young again. Sean is intermittently listening to the instructions. He is smiling ear to ear and could not wait to start the race.

The 777-marathon charter jet then took the group of 40 runners to Race 1 – Novo, Antarctica, which took 6 hours directly from South Cape Town. At the starting line, Sean made sure his timing tag is secured on his shoelaces. Antarctica is bright spanking white. Sean pulls down his sunglasses because he couldn't believe it when he saw that one of the runners is wearing tiny shorts. Then Sean hears the air horn. He paced himself at the start and tried to contain his excitement. There were drink and food stations at every 8 kms. He didn't feel like he needed to drink water as much as he did during training. He noticed thought that he's been burping and farting a lot during the race. Maybe it's the jet lag he thought. At 21st km, Sean finds himself smiling while he looked at his watch. He knows he can finish the race in 4 ½ hours. His timing tag did a double beep. Sean finished at 4 hours, 27 minutes, and 45 seconds.

Runners must provide their own food outside of the charter flights. The organisers of the marathon advised the runners where they could get some food. Sean is so surprised to find a place to eat with lots of seafood and brown rice. A lady in her 30s went passed Sean's table and said, "Those brown rice must be grown in Australia." Sean smiled and said, "It could be." The lady introduced herself. "I'm Annie, you were just ahead of me at the race." Annie joined Sean during dinner. Two more runners also joined their table.

It's a six-hour flight back to Cape Town for Race 2. Sean is feeling a bit heavy on the stomach. Perhaps the seafood? The brown rice? He ignored it and went to sleep. Five hours later, his stomach woke him.

He's got gastro. He drunk a big glass of water with a tbsp of apple cider vinegar (ACV). He took his list out of controllable/uncontrollable. Sean wrote on the controllable side – *The Power of Showing Up Each Time!* He smiles as he recalls him saying that to his clients all the time. Now he must apply that to himself, especially when the alarm clock goes off!

Race 2. The runners are chatting about the fact that they don't understand why Race 1 should have been in Cape Town and Race 2 in Antarctica. Before anyone could state a legitimate reason, they heard the air horn. It's a stark contrast to the Antarctic race. Cape Town melts the ice still under Sean's skin. He paced himself as usual. Sunglasses on, Annie waved at Sean and said Hi. Annie's high pitch voice and infectious energy got Sean running a little faster. Annie said, "Come on, mate! Are you going to let me beat you this time?" Sean just laughed out loud. His timing beeped. Finished at 4 hours, 45 minutes, and 49 seconds (4:45:49). Sean looked dejected as he saw Annie looking relaxed chatting to the other runners who have already finished. Annie's Australian accent stood out among the crowd. Sean laughs while catching his breath, when the Argentinian runner said that his Kiwi accent sounds like Annie's accent.

The 40 runners have become very supportive of each other. They were often seen laughing like a big family. Most of the runners are Caucasian. There were 4 runners from Asia, 2 from Africa and 2 from South America. About 60% of the runners are male.

Sean felt so drained after Race 2 and slept like a baby while the charter jet took them across to Perth, Australia. Annie invited the group to join her and her Australian family who organised a BBQ dinner prior to the race at dawn the following morning. About half of the runners are keen to go. The others said "no thanks" as they wanted to sleep early.

Sean didn't have the intention to join the BBQ. He didn't go to bed early either. Instead, he went for a short stroll. He is very hungry. He knew he needed to be careful with what he eats. It's 8.30pm, he presumes that most restaurants will be closing their kitchens soon. Then he saw a truck pulled over on the side of the road and he saw the driver carrying a large box of fresh produce. Sean crossed the road and followed the driver. The driver entered the back of the restaurant. Sean entered the front door of the restaurant. It's his lucky night; they have one small table available. He could see the kitchen steaming with busy chefs dressed in white. Sean sat and scanned the menu. He decided to eat light. Quinoa with sweet potato, asparagus, and zucchini. Perfect he thought, all the complex carbs he needs for the next race. He politely asked the waiter to ask the chef to use less oil.

Sean took his time eating his meal. He then sat at the bar and asked the barman politely if he could have a big glass of water with a tbsp of ACV. The barman laughed and said, "Well, there's a first time for everything!" Sean explained that he is doing a marathon at 5am by the botanical gardens by Mt Eliza. He's just trying to avoid burping and farting too much during the race. The barman said, "Fair enough, Mate. Just let me go to the kitchen and get you your special drink, okay?" Sean could see the barman through the glass kitchen window, joyfully making jokes about Sean's farting at the race. The effeminate barman returned with a tall glass of water with ACV as if he is dancing and hands it over to Sean. Sean took out his wallet, and the barman said, "Oh, it's okay, mate, this one's on the house for making all of us laugh."

One of the chefs walked over to the bar as he takes off his white uniform. The chef jokes, "I heard you're doing boom booms while running a marathon." Sean laughs and says, "I don't know what I'm eating that makes me do that." The chef said, "It could be the dairy combined with starchy carbs." Sean said, "It's funny you say that. We've been served carbonara pasta at our charter flights." The chef said, "It's likely the dairy in the pasta. My mum used to do a lot of boom booms, but it stopped since I started serving her the plant-based cheese I've been making." Sean said, "Really?" The chef said, "And my mum seemed to have reversed her diabetes after a few months." Sean's eyes lit up and said, "Wait, how can that happen?" The chef said, "Oh, don't take my word for it. I've had to close down my restaurant in Sydney last time I said that. I must emphasise to you that that's just my mum's experience."

Sean insisted, "Wait, I'd like to know more about how your mum did it." The chef said, "Look mate, I'm just here in Perth for two days to help my mate in this restaurant. I needed to be in a different environment hoping that I could think clearly about my situation in Sydney."

Sean said, "It's okay. I understand. I'm a lawyer." The chef said, "Oh great! I hope you don't sue me for saying the words – reverse diabetes!"

Sean said, "Oh, no, no, no! I meant I have pre-diabetes, and I am doing everything in my power to better my health. I'm really curious to find out as to what your mum did to get better." Sean and the chef exchanged phone numbers and social media details, mutually agreeing that they could help each other out.

The chef asked Sean why he's doing the marathon. Sean said he wanted to lose weight, sort out his pre-diabetes and that it's fun. Sean could feel in his gut that he's only trying to convince himself.

Before Sean went to sleep, he added a column on his controllable/uncontrollable sheet. He added a 'WHY' column. Sean stared at the page for 10 minutes. Then he wrote: *Because I want to change. And so that I can show my loved ones and my clients, that change is possible, that anything is possible, for those who really want it.*

Sean went to sleep hopeful.

Sean is at Race 3. It's dark at dawn and Sean's eyes are sparkling with light. He paced himself during the first 10 kms. Then he could feel his shoes tapping on the white lines on the road, faster and faster.

Sean is so wrapped. Approaching at the finish line, he knew this would be his best time ever: 4:15:02!
The group did not have time to rest in Australia. Their rest is inside the charter jet while flying to go to Race 4 – Dubai. Four hours before the race, Sean asked for pasta with greens, without the carbonara sauce! Sean flew through race 4. With higher humidity in Dubai, he drank

more water, this time with Celtic salt to make him more hydrated right through into his mitochondria. Sean wipes his sweat off his forehead. His eyes went a bit blurry, then at the finish line, he could not believe his eyes: 4:05:00!

While waiting for their next flight, Sean rang the chef and left a message. There's so much cheer in Sean's voice. His message said:

Hello, Yoshi! This is Sean, the marathon runner you met in Perth. You wouldn't believe it, mate! I didn't feel a single fart during the race! I think your 'no dairy trick' worked for me! Listen, I managed to get hold of a good lawyer in Sydney who could help you re-open your restaurant again. Call me back, Yoshi! Bye!

Chapter 12 – Anchor Me

Alisa Torres approached the man in the digger and politely asked him if they could stop digging while she did her recording in one corner of Lake Bito's black sand.

Man: Sorry, Iha. We've been instructed to dig as fast as we can.
Alisa: Um.
Alisa heard a whisper within her.
Alisa: Pwede po, ask your supervisor, please?
The man sighs: Okay, Iha.

Supervisor: Iha, you shouldn't be here during this time. It's not safe for you.
Alisa: Even for just five minutes po, please.
Supervisor: Show me where you are recording. Where is your camera?
Alisa showed the supervisor while her camera is on.
Supervisor: Okay, 5 minutes, so long as you don't capture any of the trucks and diggers. And show me what you've recorded before you leave.
Alisa: Thank you, po.

The supervisor gave his hand signal to stop the crew. Alisa pressed the red button to start recording. She closed her eyes for a few seconds to find her centre. She asked the crew to turn off all their lights. She took her jacket off, played a symphonic song and danced completely from within her Soul. The crew were quiet as real art unfolded right before their eyes. They had light tears in their eyes as if they were enlightened. Perhaps Alisa reminded them of their daughters, mothers, sisters, nieces. None of them even though of taking their phones out to take a photo or video Alisa's dancing. Then, her five minutes is up. Alisa showed the supervisor what she recorded.

Supervisor: Wow, that's looks great, Iha, you look like you're flying there. What is it for?

Alisa: It will be part of my artistic portfolio to apply for performance shows. I want to dance all over the world.
Supervisor: Good luck, Iha!

The supervisor did his hand signal to the crew. Alisa hears the truck reversing.

Alisa felt crisp air on her skin. She cupped her palms, crossed her arms and inside her dress, she put her palms concave to her shoulders. There's silence within her, like hugging self-love. Then, suddenly, she felt warmth around her. She looked up to the sky and said, "Cielo. Sky. Heaven. Lake Bito is heaven on earth. Why are they digging it?"

Alisa watched her recording and said, "Mission accomplished." She then put her camera away. While she walks, she plans to cook champorado for the priests for breakfast this morning.

Alisa felt a whisper within her – "Look back." She saw how much sand has been dug and sucked out in the last 15 minutes. She paused for a moment. She spotted some Maras Vetiver grass and kneeled down to hide behind it. She started recording the digging. By then, first light started to show through.

Alisa got back to her room. She saved both videos in her laptop. She also saved them in microSDXC card. She deleted them from her camera.

Alisa started to cook champorado. The retired priests sent feedback to the manager that the glutinous rice in the champorado is making them constipated. So, Alisa cooked it with black rice instead. She used medjool dates instead of white sugar. Though the manager said not to use too many dates as they are expensive having been imported from Saudi.

Once the champorado is cooled down, she served one bowl to each of the priests. Alisa is using a soup spoon to feed Father Joel.
Father Joel: I thought I saw you leaving early this morning. Or maybe I was dreaming.

Alisa: Yes, that was me, Father. I went to Lake Bito to record my dancing.
Father Joel: How did you go?
Alisa paused: Um.

The other priests, Father Edmundo (Father Eddie), looked at Alisa.
Father Eddie jokingly said: Alisa, you're not keeping a secret from us, are you?

Alisa while half smiling: I recorded my dancing. Kaya lang po, there were trucks and diggers there. They're digging a whole lot of sand, Father. They also have this like a giant hose sucking in the sand. I should've asked them what for.

Father Eddie chuckles and slaps the edge of the table: Ah! Is that where they're digging? I've been reading about it and wondered where they would dig next?

Alisa: Oh, you know about this, Father?
Father Eddie: Let me explain, anak (child). They're taking the sand to China and Australia.
Alisa: But can't they use their own sand?
Father Eddie: They use river and lake sand to make cement blocks to build their cities.
Alisa: But they have lots of beaches there so they can use their own sand.
Father Eddie: Beach sand is round and would not hold together when cement is produced. River and lake sand have sharp edges, so they are more useful to make the cement durable. Our black sand is so high in demand that China and Australia are buying it from us.
Alisa: But that is ruining our town. There are massive holes there, Father.
Father Eddie: I know, anak. River sand is being dug up from places like Vietnam, India and Indonesia too. If you think there are drug dealers here in Leyte, there is a mafia of sand diggers that's been here for five years before we even knew they exited. They've been digging during dawn.
Alisa: Well, can we discuss this with the mayor?

Father Eddie: Anak, there is no point. We've had issues like this for decades. Many of us tried to save our environment. But the people on top and business groups are too powerful. It's best to keep quiet to keep all of us safe.

Alissa stared at Father Joel for a moment.

Bedtime. Alisa is drying her hair with a big towel. Her phone rang. It's her father ringing from New Zealand. He told her the news that, him, Alisa's mother, and Alisa's younger sister, Rebecca, are moving to Melbourne, Australia. A decision based on selling their over-priced house in Auckland and use the net profit from sale proceeds to purchase a reasonably priced house in Melbourne which would make them mortgage-free. Alisa's father mentioned that Alisa will have her own bedroom with ensuite bathroom and walk-in wardrobe in Melbourne.

Alisa: Thank you, Daddy.
Alisa's father, Carlo: I miss you, anak. I hope you can join us in our new home.
Alisa: But what about my criminal record, Daddy?
Carlo: Don't worry, we know a good lawyer who can help you. Besides, you've been clean for the last six years, right?
Alisa answering adamantly: Yes, of course, Daddy.

Alisa immediately though of making chamomile tea. As her tears drop down her high cheeks, walking towards the kitchen, there sat Father Joel, already having the same tea.

Father Joel: I thought you might be having trouble sleeping too. What else are you crying for, anak?
Alisa: Daddy would like me to move to Australia with them. It would be good to be with my family again. What do you think I should do, Father?
Father Joel: It is up to you. Maybe go and visit them first and then, see what your Soul asks you to do.
Alisa: What about Lake Bito, Father?
Father Joel looking directly at Alisa's tired eyes: Anak, Lake Bito needs your help, but you cannot do it alone. You must seek help from others.

Alisa was surprised with Father's Joel's answer. She presumed that he would say the same as Father Eddie, since Father Joel kept quiet the whole time Father Eddie was saying that there is nothing we can do.

Father Joel handed Alisa a white rosary and said: Here, pray and you will have a clear answer sometime in the morning. Please remember Alisa, that when we act on what our Soul ask us to do, everything else that is irrelevant will just naturally fall away.

Alisa put the rosary on top of her bookshelf. She thinks she could not pray the rosary another second, she thinks it's repeatedly boring.

Alisa woke up. It's her day off from work. She washed up and decide to go to Lake Bito. Her big toe felt a little stone. She stepped over her rosary which must have fallen on the floor. She picked it up and noticed that under it, there is an orange small sticky note. It said, 'Simple, Small, NOW!' Alisa presumed that it must be from one of the priests. She put the rosary and the note in her pocket.

At the lake, she noticed that the sand level is lower. The diggers must have smoothened and levelled out the sand before they left.

She was going to practice some of her dance steps. She noticed a woman sitting right in the middle. She seems to be meditating. The woman felt a gaze perception but ignored it. When the woman finished meditating, she stood up and saw Alisa looking at her.

Woman: Hi, do you live here?
Alisa: Yes, yes, I do. I noticed you meditating, and I wondered what that feels like.
Woman: Oh, I feel like I have some clarity afterwards.
Alisa: I used to pray the rosary, but I often find no guidance whatsoever.
Woman: Perhaps, you can do both. Pray the rosary with more heart, rather than just saying the words. Perhaps do some visualisation of your intentions while you pray and do it while breathing slowly. You know, you could do both. It doesn't have to be one or the other.
Alisa: Thank you, I shall try that.

Woman: I'm here in the Philippines for a few days to train farmers how to get WWOOFers.
Alisa: Is that Aussie accent I hear?
Woman laughing slightly: Yeah, how did you know?
Alisa: My family and I lived in New Zealand for a while but they're moving to Melbourne soon.
Woman: Oh, I'm from Melbourne. You should come and visit. I'm Amelia, by the way.
Alisa: I'm Alisa. I could perhaps move to Melbourne, but I like it here.
Amelia: Perhaps you could stay with your family there for a few months and the rest of the time here. You know, it doesn't have to be one place or another. You could have the best of both worlds. It's up to you.

Amelia and Alisa exchanged phone numbers and social media details.

What Alisa is unaware of is that the Soul of Martin Vordr has been whispering to her Soul:

Ask the digger's supervisor.

After her dance recording, Martin hugged her to keep her warm.

Look back. So, Alisa can record the digging.

Martin anchored her along the hallway to the kitchen as she cries to go and make chamomile tea.

Now Alisa sits on the black sand, holding her white rosary, meditating, and envisioning her hopes for Lake Bito. Strangely, she felt warmth all over her back.

Martin hugs her and whispers: *Stay here, Alisa, please stay.*

While Alisa drives back to the retirement home, she took the wrong turn. She was hitting her forehead with her palm as she took another wrong turn.

Alisa said to herself: "Mama Mia, Alisa, you must be so tired!"

Then she noticed, she just went passed the municipio. She parked her car and tidied up herself. At reception, she asked if it's possible to speak with the mayor.

Receptionist: Do you have an appointment, Miss?
Alisa: Not yet.
Receptionist: Wait, there's been a cancellation. Let me see. Do you have an ID, Miss?
Alisa: Here you go.
Receptionist: What would you like to discuss with the mayor, Miss?
Alisa: It's about Lake Bito.
Receptionist: Okay, let me call the mayor first. I need to let you know that his office has a camera and it's continually recording.
Alisa: That's fine.

The receptionist proceeded to ask the mayor for permission.

The security guards checked Alisa's bag, her clothes and then she went through security scanners as if she is going through airport security.

The guards led Alisa to the mayor's office.

Chapter 13 – Humanity is so Young

Martin Vordr is floating on Lake Bito, thinking how he can stay on Earth. He wondered if he could swim as fast as he could run. He almost parted the lake in the middle. He stopped because he noticed he was disturbing the other creatures in the lake. Three Dalmatia pelicans seem to tell him off by the way they were flapping their wings towards him.

Martin rests on top of the lake. He lit up the whole area. People in the province presumed the light coming from the lake is a reflection from the full moon.

Massive dark cloud then covered the moon. Martin turned down his white fire-like image way down. He didn't want to attract attention from members of the public. Martin felt peace for a moment. Then he started planning how he could help Alisa further.

Martin closed his eyes. It's completely dark. He sees nothing, though he feels an enormous amount of love, but he is not sure where it's coming form, what for and who for.

Then, four bright light images of masculine men surround him. His eyes are still closed so he presumed that he must be dreaming. He wondered: *So, my Soul still have dreams?*

One of the four men of Light: Martin, we are here to guide you back to the Light.
Martin: Thank you but I would like to stay here.

Martin in his thoughts labelled the four men of Light as 'Elins' which means shining bright sunbeam.

Elin 1 (Kristian): Your stay would have to come with good intentions and good deeds.
Martin: I'm helping Alisa save Lake Bito.

Elin 2 (Gustav): We both know that your intention of falling in love with Alisa is more than help her save the lake.
Martin stood up with a tone of anger in his voice: My life was taken away from me.

The Elins made a chain by holding each other's hands and they surround Martin. Then, Martin saw his mother in Norway. She's crying while going through Martin's medals which he accomplished from his iron man races.

Elin 3 (Olav): We need your help to allow your mother to grieve and move on.
Elin 4 (Aleksander): So that your Soul can move on too.

Martin can run and swim fast, but he could not fly. The Elins held and lifted him up and they flew to Norway.

Martin hugged his mum and with his fingers, gently brushed her fringe away from her forehead as she lays in bed. Martin could hear all her thoughts. They're all in a form of questions: *Why Martin? Why so young?* Martin tried to answer her questions through her spirit.

Martin: Only God has the answer. For 26 years, I received your love, Mamma. I thank you for that.
Martin's mum: But I have so much more love to give.
Martin: There are many others who would gladly receive your love.

For the first time since Martin passed away, his mother fell in deep sleep. She slept continuously for 9 hours. The next morning, she made phone calls to the local schools. She put her name down to volunteer to teach young children how to read in Norsk and in English.

Martin noticed that only two of the Elins are around. After half an hour, the other two Elins arrived.

Kristian: Our mission here is to take you back to the Light.
Martin: I understand.

Aleksander: We have a message from the higher Divine if you still want to stay on Earth.
Martin looked intensely at the Elins as he waits for the message.
Olav: The Divine require you to protect and guide a group of people. You must gather these individuals into a group and do your best to protect and guide them to accomplish their mission.
Martin: And what is their mission?
Gustav: The story of humanity is still young and humans are yet to learn so much. Humans are like toddlers making a mess of their own world. One of the best ways to get humans to clean up their mess is for them to realise that we are all inter-beings.
Martin: Inter-beings?
Gustav: Humans' tendency is to only take care of themselves. We are here to teach humans that the Earth, the non-human animal kingdom, the plant kingdom, the ocean, the mushrooms, the microbes, the rocks, are all interconnected. The mission is to have humans move away from the ideology of being separate. Separate from one country to another, separate from Nature, as a separate higher being from other living things.
Martin: Wow! Which group am I protecting and guiding?
Olav: You will know as you go. Each step will lead to another.

The Elins flew towards southeast.

Martin sighs with relief and whispers "I can stay." While thinking he has a big job at hand.

Martin watched his mum teach little children how to read. When she finished reading, the children were asking all sorts of funny questions. Martin's mother is laughing once again. Martin kissed his mother's forehead. When he was young, it was the other way around.

Martin started running and had no idea where to. He saw some lights and some smoke through a large forest. He stopped at what looks like a native community. He saw a man, somewhat in his mid-20s, trying to inhale the hallucinogen yopo.

It's midday, Martin thinks that it must be the first time this young man is trying yopo. The tribesmen laugh as the young man coughs. The young man then said, "No more! This is not for me!"

The forest is suddenly quiet. It got dark quickly, and heavy rain started to fall. They are at the northernmost part of the Amazon. The young man quickly put his dark raincoat on and proceeded to cover all his equipment.

The young man is Michael Johnson. He studied hard at university as he promised in his letter to his mother. Michael is a microbiologist and has been assigned to do biocultural research on the Yanomami tribe. A half-Yanomami himself, Michael's quest is to honour the Yanomami heritage and its biological legacy.

Michael is often challenged by Nature as he tried to protect the microbiome samples which he himself collects from members of the tribe. He is often nervous and frantic about keeping his delicate samples and equipment dry. Michael must go on fragile boats often along the river to find more members of the tribe.

Michael made it to his base; he settled and went to bed.

Martin's main job is not just to protect and guide Michael. Martin is outside, speaking to one of the Elins.

Olav: Guide Michael to find his mother. Without his reconnection with her, Michael would self-sabotage.

Chapter 14 – How Do I Find You

Michael's eyes are half-closed. He can hear the whole tribe chanting. They surround him chanting and blowing smoke towards him. Michael feels a pounding headache. His high fever is making him shake and sweat.

Michael whispers to himself, "I had three doses of the vaccine. It's supposed to be effective for 12 months. I guess I got a different strain of malaria." One of the chiefs of the tribe is shouting to the clouds. Perhaps he is angry that most people presume that malaria is from the natives. That natives get blamed for it even though it's the miners that spread it within their community and the disease are still killing members of the Yanomami tribe.

A bare-breasted woman is helping Michael sit up against the wall. She has been stirring a big pot of soup. The woman prepares soup everyday in preparation to serve to anyone who gets sick within their community. The pot of soup caught Michael's attention. The woman made the soup with bark scrapings and torn-up marantaceous leaves. She cooked it in the fire and extracted the juice. She then took out a big wooden bowl and pounded a big ripe papaya, including all the seeds. With her bare hands, she took out the papaya skin. She pounded the papaya flesh ensuring that the seeds are all squashed with the flesh. She then added the papaya mix to the bark and leaves soup. The woman slowly fed Michael the soup. Due to the papaya seeds, the soup is very bitter, leaving a sweet and earthy aftertaste. The chanting finished. The woman helped Michael lay down on the woven mat.

The woman went back to her part of the yano which is about 10 metres away from Michael. At 3am, the woman was woken up by a light showing through the gap of her roof. She covered the gap with some long plantain leaves. The woman is confused as she could not see the full moon while the sky is clear. The night is so quiet that the woman

Rebecca overhead their conversation.

Rebecca: Mum, Dad, you know you used to let Alisa, and I watch 'The Lion King' like a million times?
Carlo: Yes, what are you trying to say, Rebecca?
Rebecca: Well, do you think that if Mufasa and Sarabi kept Simba safe with them for long, do you think Simba would even try to be brave?
Cora: That's a very good point, anak.
Carlo: Well, I would like us to be a family again, even for just a short period of time.
Rebecca: Daddy, you used to read me 'The Alchemist'. It says there that love has no ownership. Maybe it's time to let Alisa live her own life.
Cora looking at Carlo: She's right you know.

Alisa arrived at the Melbourne Tullamarine Airport. Carlo shows Alisa her well-made Tuscan-based bed, surrounded with some indoor plants, a study space in one corner with a big vase of her favourite flowers - big-faced sunflowers, some new linen clothes and cotton pyjamas in her walk-in wardrobe and rose-infused soap in her own bath and shower.

Alisa: I like this smaller house better, Daddy. I feel much closer to all of you. There was no need for such a large house we had in Auckland, did we?

After a restful night, the family drove to Lakes Entrance for 4 ½ hours. Had some lunch, ate lots of donuts, and drove back. The family talked about people they know, politics and the travels they hope to do.
Alisa feels very comfortable with her family. At day 5, she felt bored. That night she messaged Amelia. They agreed to meet at the Flinders St Station.

Amelia: So, you still meditate with your white rosary?
Alisa gently punching Amelia's right shoulder: Heck yeah! It's making me brave. Thanks to you!
Amelia: That'd girl!
Alisa: My parents and my sister are at church now. My dad's a bit disappointed that I didn't go with them.
Amelia: D'you want to get some gelato? We can go to Piccolina.

could hear Michael moaning. She carried a bowl of her soup and picked a fresh ripe papaya on her way to Michael's part of the yano.

The yano in the Yanomami community are not stand-alone dwellings. They are connected and structured as a large circular community dwelling. The tribe traditionally build them this way so that they can easily help each other. The yano communal dwelling is also called the shabono.

For an hour, the woman slowly fed Michael the soup. Michael slept though for five hours. Everyone in the community is quietly doing their work early in the morning. The children walk pass to check in on Michael to ensure he is okay.

Michael woke up with his woven mat wet with sweat, though his headache is gone. As he stood up, he immediately heard his stomach glug. He runs to the tribe's designated toilet. He smells the stench of his poop, with traces of the sweet smell of papaya.

Five minutes later, he could smell bread being cooked by the tribeswomen. They are cooking casava flat bread over a round stone, ash and burning wood.

Michael went for a quick swim in the river.

As the tribe gathered to have the flat bread, Michael found the woman who cared for him the night before to thank her. He started asking the woman and the other woman around her who might know his mother, Marima. The name does not mean anything to the women as Yanomami do not usually have names. Michael started showing them a photo of his mother and him while he was little, with a Californian playground in the background. The woman tried to explain to Michael that she will walk far and wide to help him find his mother. Michael is aware that there are around 30,000 plus members of the Yanomami tribe. Michael indicated to her that he will go with her. A few of the tribesmen volunteered to help as well. The chief warned it could be very dangerous as they could end up in another part of the Yanomami community where it's leaders could start a war if they were approached the wrong way.

Michael's plan is to also collect microbiome samples if tribe leaders allow him to do so.

At night, while Michael slowly rocks inside his woven hammock, he recalls his conversation with his father, Chris, before he left for the Amazon.

Chris: Mike, what's the point in trying to find your mother? Firstly, it's very dangerous down there. Not just from the diseases you could contract, but also from the people there. Modern day pirates would kill for no reason at all. You know, while I was there, about two months before I met your mom, I witnessed some pirates hold up a group of people from a United Nations voyage. They were in a yacht with environmentalist from New Zealand. The men from the yacht refused to hand over their guns to the pirates. So, the pirates shot and killed everyone in the yacht, including the women. I hid and run through the forest to get some help, but it was too late. The yacht was gone by the time the authorities got there.

Michael: I'm sorry that this expedition greatly worries you, Dad. You know, I must do this otherwise I will wonder for the rest of my life. One day, I will have children, and you know what? If I don't find Mom, one of my children will.

Chris: You were too little to understand when your Mom left. She abandoned us, Mike. Like my biological mother gave me up 2 days after I was born.

Michael: Come on, Dad! You know Mom looked after us really well for so many years before she left. You know, I remember her looking so broken a few months before she left. She was so sad every single day. That, I remember. She must have had an extremely good reason to leave.

Chris sighs and looks away from Michael and said nothing.

Chris: I've drawn up a map, a list of people and list of words that will be useful while you are there. I knew I couldn't stop you. I feel like you're abandoning me too.

Michael: That's not fair, Dad.

Michael fell asleep cocooned inside his hammock. He fell into a dream state. A calm river that becomes wild as soon as he steps in it. He vividly saw the Misk Peak as if it is right in front of him. He walked passed a giant tree with its trunk painted with long black squiggles and red circles with eyes in the middle. He swum through the snake-shaped part of the Orinoco River.

Early in the morning, Michael gathered his gear, equipment, the map and the lists from his dad. The tribesmen have already prepared the boat. Michael's sudden thought as he hopped into the boat is how is he going to find his mother in a tribal land that is twice the size of Switzerland. He looked at the determined woman and tribesmen, somehow, his doubt dissipated.

During their first two days of their journey, the group took a few breaks and harvested edible grubs from fallen rotting trees. Then they found another tribal dwelling. The tribe politely welcomed them, and they had a safe place to sleep.

On the third day, midway to the Casiquiare Canal, relentless rain was pounding on their boat. Michael took his well-sealed equipment and held it against his chest under his grey raincoat. The continuous thunder and lightning shook Michael's nerves each time. He though he saw a head of an anaconda with horns float in the river. He then had a flashback of his mother tucking him into bed when he was five. Michael could not tell the difference between the saltiness of the rain dripping from the hood of his raincoat from the saltiness of his own tears.

The rain stops. They dragged the boat at a riverbank. Michael turned around and witnessed the most beautiful sunset he has ever seen. Purply blue sky with brush painted like clouds of golden turmeric. The sunset is reflected in the water and the colours seemed to dance with lighter shades of gold. Along the horizon, there were silhouettes of trees on the right side of his view. Just before the sun disappeared, Michael saw bright lights showing through the golden clouds. The group are now in the state of Amazonas. Michael is glad that he also has a visa for Venezuela.

Michael sleeps through the night and woke up alone. From a distance, he could hear a woman speaking to another woman. Michael walked over closer to them. The other woman stood up and slowly walked toward Michael. She started crying. So did Michael. They just both knew. The bond of a good mother and her child is never broken. No matter how far apart they are. Michael and his mother held each other. Marima's right ear is pressed against Michael's chest, right where his heart his.

Michael is interchangeably saying: I missed you so much, Mom. I'm so happy I found you.

Michael looked at his diminutive mother with so much love and Marima looked up at him with so much joy in her eyes.

Marima tried to explain why she left California. She then tried to explain to Michael by drawing on the river sand. Michael is so amazed at how good his mother drew his father's image on the sand. Then Marima drew a woman with long curly hair, kissing his father. Marima then drew an image of herself with her short upside-down bowl-like shaped hair, with tears flowing through her cheeks.

Michael knew how sad his mom was. But he didn't know that his mom was broken because his father was unfaithful.

Marima explained through her drawing that she wanted to take Michael back to the Amazon. But she lost that fight. She then explained that she knew that the Xipiripë (Yanomami spirit) would bring them back together.

Marima has facial piercing. She has a long stick horizontally pierced through the columella of her noise. Two short sticks poking out beside the corners of her lips and another one through her chin.

The tribesmen arrive back from a day's hunting. The two women started cooking. After the men cleaned their hunting tools, they started cleaning the village. In the Yanomami culture, it is the men who does the cleaning.

While Michael sat in his hammock, his mother came and threw a big slab of cooked meat towards him. Michael caught it with both hands. It's a 1.5-foot-long part of a boa constrictor. Michael used his fingers slowly, while letting steam out, to check if it's cooked through. He smiled at his mother. Michael is very hungry and ate it, thinking to himself:

I'm surprised; it has an oily texture like scallops.

Chapter 15 – I Hug Your Innocent Fear

Amelia flew via Scoot from the Philippines to Melbourne with a layover in Singapore. She arrived around midday and took Uber home.

At 4am, she had pain in her lower stomach. She got up to urinate and opened the shutters slightly to let some moonlight in. She noticed there's some blood with her urine. She didn't want to turn on the light, but she did, to confirm that it is blood. ''Blast!'', she said. She took some Panadol and went back to bed holding her stomach with her knees bent as she tries to sleep on her side.

Fortunately, she's not rostered at the farm the next day. Amelia went to see her GP. Confirmed – UTI (Urinary Tract Infection). Her GP said it's mostly common with women who often eat pork while overseas. Amelia explained that her pain is 8 out of 10. Her GP gave her some antibiotics.

The infection subsided after a few days. Though Amelia noticed she's frequently going to the toilet.

For eight months, Amelia was progressively getting stomach crumps. She put that down to her monthly period. She then caught on, that she's also getting the crumps two weeks before the onset of her period.

Marching out of the clinic. Amelia exhales with a big sigh, looking like she's about to swear. She's been diagnosed with IBS (Irritable Vowel Syndrome). In her hand is an A4 sheet of list of food she must be careful of ingesting.

Around this time, Carlo, Alisa's father, got up at dawn. He is in Dannemora, Auckland, New Zealand. He is preparing their house for auction at 10am.

At 9am, Rohit from Ray White real estate was ringing their doorbell. He prepares the documentation with Carlo and Cora.

All is set and ready to go. Several young couples turned up. Also, individuals in their 50s. Plus other real estate agents representing overseas buyers. Soon, some of the neighbours arrived.
The auctioneer rang a bell to get everyone's attention. Holding a wooden hammer in his right hand, he starts the auction. It started slowly which made Carlo and Cora nervous. The bidding at this time is $50k lower than what they wanted. Then a couple in their late 30s are running towards the driveway. Luckily, then had already pre-registered and they apologised for being late. The bidding then progressed – rapidly! It was between the couple who were late and a man in his 50s. Then, the auctioneer shouted, "Going once, going twice, sold to the young couple for NZD1.46 million.

Alisa's parents are extremely happy with the result of the auction. Smiles are all around. All parties got what they wanted. Carlo and Cora are encircled by their neighbours congratulating them. The neighbours are also happy now that they have some idea of what their own properties are worth.

Carlo excused himself to call Alisa. He left a message.

Cora served wine, cheese and crackers, coffee and casava cake, to their guests, friends, and neighbours to celebrate. They sat around the outdoor table. One of Carlo's friends stood up and cheerfully said, "Cheers to Carlo and Cora's new adventures in Australia!"

In flight with Qantas, Carlo sits in the middle isle. Cora and their younger daughter, Rebecca, sit together on the left side of the plane. Carlo is in deep thought. He left his food uneaten for the last 15 minutes.

A man in his mid-50s sits next to Carlo jokingly said, "Are you going to eat that?"

Carlo: Um, I'm not hungry, here, I'll have the bread and butter, you have this."

Carlo handed the man the main meal still covered with foil.
Man: Oh no, I was just kidding, mate.
Carlo laughs: I insist, you look like you're still hungry.
Man laughs: Thanks mate. I'm one of those people who can't hide how they feel.
Carlo: I'm Carlo, by the way.
Man: I'm Tim. Are you Filo?
Carlo laughs: Cannot hide it!

While they eat:
Tim: Why are you so deep in thought?

Carlo thinking for a few seconds that he can be honest with this guy thinking he won't see him again anyway.

Carlo: Um, you know, New Zealand is such a beautiful country, I think I would have stayed if the cost of living wasn't so high.
Tim: Oh, so you're from Auckland? I lived there too, on the North Shore.
Carlo: I'm a bit sad I've left behind some really good friends there.
Tim: You know, when I moved to Aussie 30 years ago, I realised which of my old friends are real friends and which are just deal friends. During the first five years, I've had to let go of my deal friends.

Carlo: What d'you mean by deal friends?
Tim: Well, they tend to be risk averse. They tend to want you to stay the way you are. They try to discourage you from moving but they don't do it directly.
Carlo: Oh.
Tim: They tend to compare New Zealand versus Australia. Though I never understood the validity of their comparison when they've never lived in Australia. So, they tend to watch the news and believe everything they hear is permanent, like it's forever. They tend to think that Aussies give Kiwis a hard time, but to be honest, mate, I've been given so many opportunities here since I moved.
Carlo: Okay. I can think of a couple of friends that may fall in that 'deal' category. There's also some kind of guilt and shame built in when they discourage you from moving.

Tim: I don't mean to be negative, mate. I'm sure you have lots of real friends.
Carlo: Oh yes! I definitely know which friends of ours accepts me and my wife's sense of adventure.

Tim: I've had to let go of a dear friend a few years ago. Mate, you wouldn't believe it. We were such best buddies. We liked the same movies, clothes, cars, you name it. But when I started to broaden my horizon, change my taste, my style. He started being resentful. He wasn't doing it directly. He does it by being sarcastic and being a kill joy in anything I say.
Carlo: Oh my God! That's what a couple of our friends are doing.

Tim: I think they are doing it unconsciously. Not realising they are trying to sabotage your faith that you will do your best to make it work. In a nutshell, they are trying stop you from evolving.

Carlo: You mean, they're trying to make you the same as they are. Where they think they are safe. Like it's some kind of deal. And we broke that deal.

Tim: You nailed it in the head, mate. Listen, I'm no psychologist, but I think they try to pretend that they want to make you secure and safe, but to be honest, they couldn't face the truth that you have the guts to take risks, and they don't. That's why they hold on to their nationalistic ideology. Deep down, they know that you will have some challenges and fun along the way. They resent you for that because you are ready to evolve, and they don't have the balls to change and grow.

Carlo: So, Tim, 30 years huh? You still think you made the right decision?

Tim: You could say that mate. I'm not Aussie nor am I Kiwi. I'm just me, with lots of interesting different life experiences. I take the best of both worlds. I think if I'd stayed in New Zealand for the last 30 years, my perspective wouldn't be as wide as it is now. Even if I was forced to go back to New Zealand when I get old. I know I've evolved. I can get excited and tell my grandchildren stories they would not get from books or the internet. I've met people from my primary school 30 years later and they're still working for the same organisation, and they still talk the same way. I could even predict their narrative. Quite boring, really.

Carlo: I'm so glad you're sitting next to me.
Tim laughs: Likewise, mate! You gave me your food!

At the baggage claim area, Carlo run into Tim again.

Carlo jokingly: I was hoping I won't see you again.
Tim: Hey Carlo, remember to let go of your deal friends who practice tribal shaming and guilt. Their words will eat away at you. Stay out of their 'cultish' circle, okay?
Carlo smiles with respect: Keep being adventurous, mate!

Carlo and Cora rented a house in Caroline Springs, Melbourne, for eight months while their new house is being built. They've opted for a smaller property that is low maintenance in a new estate in Atherstone, a short drive to the V-Line train station. Cora can easily go to work at the Sunshine hospital and Rebecca; their younger daughter can commute to go to uni.

Cora stands barefoot on their fresh pine wooden floor. She inhales the smell of new. She went out the front door and wore her chinelas. Cora stood on their quiet street 5 metres away from the façade of their new home. She whispers to the sky, "Salamat po." She felt so much joy in her heart.

Carlo, who was the Finance Director for the Manukau Institute of Technology, shows a long sigh of relief that finally, they are mortgage-free. He joined Cora outside.

Carlo: There's one more thing to accomplish.
Cora. Alisa.
Carlo: We have enough to hire a brilliant lawyer.
Cora: Maybe that's not the real challenge. Maybe, she's established a life in the Philippines.

Alisa: You mean, ice cream?
Amelia laughs: Oh, don't let anyone hear you say that. Many Italians here would get offended.

Before Amelia and Alisa are back at the station:

Amelia: Hey, would you like to volunteer at the farm where I work? We will show you what to do and we'll cook you morning tea and lunch. We eat altogether at the farm. It will be loads of fun.

Alisa thought about it for a few seconds: Hey, why not.

Alisa got back to her parents and told them how excited she is to do something totally different and that she's glad to have started a friendship with Amelia.

Cora is disappointed that their plan to go shopping and to eat out with Alisa is no longer happening.

Alisa: I'm sorry, Mum. I don't need new clothes or shoes anyway. Volunteering will be good for me. Amelia said I can get a box of vegetables after volunteering. When I get back, maybe, you, Rebecca and I can cook dinner.

Cora: That's a good idea! Go, ask your sis.

The family had a bonding time together, cooking, having dinner and making halo-halo. They watched Netflix till late. Alisa got bored the next day and volunteered the following day at the farm.

Before bedtime, Carlo knocked on Alisa's bedroom door and sat on the side of her bed. Alisa while brushing her long hair asked her father how his new job is going.

Carlo: It's okay. I'm still getting used to the new systems. But I'm especially happy when I get my pay. You know, they pay me $40k more for a similar job that I had in Auckland. Plus, there's lots of perks.
Alisa: I'm so glad for you, Daddy.

Carlo: You know Alisa, the council is building a new public hospital by the main town here, and a new private hospital is being built next to our train station. There are so many opportunities here for you.

Alisa: Thank you, Daddy. I will think about it.

Alisa's mobile rang. It's Amelia.
Amelia: Hey Alisa, my grandpa in Moreton Bay invited me to go over this coming weekend. Apparently, there's a project happening that my grandpa is involved with, a citizen science community idea for the coral watch. Remember Amanda at the farm?
Alisa: Yeah, of course!
Amelia: Well, she's going with me. You're welcome to join us if you want. It's just over the weekend.
Alisa: Yeah, sure! Count me in. I miss being close to the water.
Amelia: We're leaving from the farm on Friday at 2pm.
Alisa: I'll meet you there.

Carlo is disappointed that Alisa could not join them to the blessing of their house this coming weekend.

Alisa saw her father having a cup of tea out at the veranda. She apologised, said goodnight to him and gave him a big hug.

Amelia, Alisa and Amanda took turns driving. Both Amelia and Amanda occasionally needed to remind Alisa to keep left. They stopped by and stayed at Amelia's mother's place in Sydney. Soon after breakfast, they drove and arrived late evening at Moreton Bay.

Rudy showed them where they can sleep. Alisa went to the bathroom and could hear Rudy and Amelia kind of whispering to each other. Alisa heard it. Rudy is not comfortable for Alisa to stay at his place overnight.

Rudy: I've never had a coloured person in my house. I don't know if I can trust her.
Amelia: For goodness's sake, Rudy! It's 2024! She's the sweetest being I know.

Alisa cut in calmly: It's okay, Amelia. I can book a hotel nearby. I'd probably be more comfortable there. And with all due respect, sir, after hearing what you said, I don't know if I can trust you.

Rudy: I'm sorry I offended you. Well, um, there's always a first time for everything. Please, stay.

Rudy had little sleep that night. Though he had everything prepared the day before.

At the Bay, Rudy is showing the girls how to use the equipment to test the water and get samples of seaweed, sand and stone and anything else they think might be relevant. Rudy gathered the girls and walked towards the building allocated for Mission Blue. Moreton Bay was chosen as a hope spot by Mission Blue a few years ago.

Rudy went to the reception and asked for Nicole, the lady who regularly works there. The new lady at the reception told Rudy that Nicole and she are in an exchange program. So, Nicole is in Costa Rica in exchange for the new lady to help look after the Moreton Bay hope spot.

New Lady: I'm Magdalena. Have you got some new samples for me, sir?
Rudy: Um, I don't think I should give this to you.
Magdalena: Oh.
Rudy: Is there somebody else?
Amelia took the samples from Rudy: It's okay, Opa. This lovely lady will look after this for us.
Amanda led Rudy outside the building.

Amelia to Magdalena: I'm so sorry. My great grandpa is just getting old.
Magdalena: I understand. I've had a few over the last two days. The elderly who want to help our environment but does not know how to interact with people of colour. Um, thank you for helping with getting some samples. Come over, I'll show you something.

Magdalena led Amelia and Alisa to an enclosed area where they are looking after three injured dugongs.

Amelia: What's happening with their skin?
Magdalena: We don't know yet. We've done lots of tests. We will release them once we know and when they are well enough. Where are you ladies from?
Amelia: I'm from Melbourne.
Alisa: My parents live in Melbourne. My home base is in the Philippines at the moment.
Magdelena: Oh, I'm trying to book an Airbnb in Melbourne so I can go at a conference there in Carlton. I still haven't received a confirmation.
Amelia: Well, if you get stuck, there is a vacant caravan at the farm where I work, if that's your kind of thing. The farm is in an urban area, so you can still catch the train to your conference.

Amelia, Alisa and Magdalena exchanged contact details.

Amelia: Oh, I received a message from Michael.
Alisa: Ooh, whose Michael? Is he cute?
Amelia laughs: It's nothing, just some dude I met at a yoga retreat.
Magdalena: Oh, I just received a message from our Costa Rican office saying some guy named Jacob is trying to get hold of me.
Alisa: Ooh, whose Jacob? Is he cute?
Magdalena laughs: Oh, I remember now, he's the guy who helped me rescue a giant turtle in Costa Rica. And yes! Super cute!
Alisa: Who? The giant turtle?

A real connection begun as they giggled like little girls.

Amelia could see Rudy's head and neck elongating on the side of the big front door.

Amelia: Oh, my Opa. He looks so tired. It's his first time interacting with 2 coloured people in one day.

Alisa laughs outload and then she gave Rudy a good long hug before they left the Mission Blue building.

Amelia traced a little tear on the side of Rudy's eyes, and also, a loving and accepting smile.

Chapter 16 – Connect to Serve

Madrid. Race 5. Sean chose another pair of running shoes. One that has more grip. The event director advised them that Madrid has many cobblestone roads, and many paths are uneven.

20 minutes before the start, the participants gathered as usual. Sean could overhear a lady with an Irish accent.

Irish Lady named Ciara: Would anyone like to volunteer to run along with me? Rich, the race director usually runs with me, but I think he needs a break.

Sean instantly thought to keep quiet.

Annie with her Australian accent: I would love to run with you, Hon!
Ciara hugs Annie: Thanks very much Annie!

Sean is running numbers in his head. He wants to do better than Race 4. He's aiming for 4 hours on the dot. He was thinking that Ciara would slow him down. He wants to keep showing his family and mates that his progress is continuous.

Annie and Ciara are pacing themselves during the first 3 kms. They're both very chatty. Like two birds you could hear in the spring all day long.

Annie: Now, you let me know if I need to slow down, okay?
Ciara: No, you let me know if I need to slow down!
The ladies laughed and hugged again.

After five kms of running:
Annie: Can I ask you a personal question?
Ciara: Shoot.
Annie: What made you blind?

Ciara: I was born blind. It was caused by congenial rubella syndrome. That's the scientific term. Basically, it's an infection while I was still unborn.
Annie: You're a remarkable person, Ciara!
Ciara: Thank you. It turns out my blindness is some kind of gift.

A friendship developed as they progressively run faster.

Finish line. Sean sighs with a frown. 4:15:00. Ten minutes slower that race 4. Sean wants to kick his own ass. In his front view is Annie and Ciara looking relaxed. They obviously finished well before him. Sean is catching his breath. He stops and puts his palms on top of his knees. He then clasps his hands as he put them on top of his head to try and catch more oxygen. He is trying to avoid Annie and Ciara. It's his opportunity to tell himself off quietly:

You're such a drongo, Sean! You pre-judged a blind person when she asked for help. All you think about is what your family and mates would think and say. See! So selfish! You know what, Sean? Your pre-diabetes could eventually lead to blindness!

Sean paused. He had some drinks and food at the event drink station. He said to himself: *Okay, lesson learnt. My WHY is not for me. It's for every person I encounter in my life.*

Inflight, Sean went to the chef and asked if he could have more vegs, no sugar and low carbs for his next meal. It was no hassle at all for the chef to adjust for his request.

Chef: How did race 5 go?
Sean: Not so good.
Chef: Why?
Sean: 10 minutes slower than race 4.
Chef: That's not bad at all. I would be happy if I could still run after race 1. So why low carb?
Sean: I'm pre-diabetic.
Chef: You know, this is how I see things. Feel free to stop me if you like. Most people tend to overlook objective reality. People with

diabetes are told to avoid sugar and carbs. Yet if you look at the world data, sugar and carbs consumption per capita is lower today than in the 1990s, but 1 in 3 of us now have diabetes. There is this island in Japan called Okinawa. Historically, it had one of the lowest rates of diabetes. Then there was a sudden upshoot in diabetes. People didn't click that the major change in that island a few months prior to the upshoot in numbers of diabetes is that half a dozen of KFC restaurants were built and was introduced to their community. They obviously love eating it. Now, you tell me. Do you think that's a coincidence? The world has demonised carbs. Most people do not know the difference between carbs from sugar and processed food and complex carbs from sweet potatoes and lentils. I think the culprit is excess animal protein that is combined with trans-fat and saturated fat.

Sean: You made some valid points there, mate. Now you know what to serve me then.
The chef tapped Sean's shoulder: You'll be right, mate. Good luck with the next race!

Fortaleza, Brazil. Race 6. The city lies at the mouth of Paheu River on the northeastern part of Brazil. It's humid. Hydration is key, Sean tells himself.
Despite the rain, the slushy road, the agonising pain in his feet, Sean feels revived and even enjoyed his run. He found Fortaleza stunning. Even on a rainy day, he had time to admire the modern city with traces of Portuguese colonial history. Sean learnt to ignore the pain from the blisters under his feet. They're probably bleeding by now.

Sean is so wrapped. 4:04:38. He goes to hug both Annie and Ciara.

Out of nowhere, for a moment, Sean thought of Yoshi, the chef from Australia.

Last race. Miami, Florida. Sean offered to run together with Ciara. Excitement is brewing throughout the town. Americans love to celebrate. All the world marathon participants are very tired. Their fatigue seems to have dissipated when they saw the community's enthusiasm. One thing is for certain. The participants have made friends for life in just a week.

The more kms the participants run, the more people turned up and cheered for them. Sean is surprised with the vibe of Miami. Thought Miami's environment seems to be stuck in the 1970s, the public seem genuinely kind and cheerful. Sean feels a strong community spirit. He is amazed at how much outdoor space Miami has for people to exercise and connect.

4 kms to the finish line, African men, women and children danced while they wear their Ugandan traditional clothes, to the beat of their drums. Most of the participants are trying to hold back their tears. Their adrenalin is higher than ever before. Their ego wants them to run faster to the finish line. Their hearts don't want this experience to end. The camera crew captured their tug-of-war of emotions.

A cameraman shouted with his Australian accent: Hey, mate, do you mind looking at the camera? Sean puts his thumb up.
Cameraman: See you at the finish line, yeah?
Sean puts his other thumb up.

Finish line. The timer tag beeped so loud as Sean and Ciara finished at the same time, with their large elastic band connecting them together. Emotions were running so high for both, and the camera crew captured it so well.

4:00:00.

Ciara could not hold her tears any longer. She held Sean so tight, they both could hardly catch their breath. Sean gave a hand signal to the camera crew to give them some space. Sean and Ciara rubbed and tapped each other's back as they hug and said to each other: Keep in touch. Especially when you're feeling vulnerable.

The participants quickly had some food and drink.

Ciara was then interviewed by the media for her newly achieved Guiness world record as the first blind person to complete the 777 challenge. Sean had an interview about his journey with pre-diabetes. Yoshi crossed Sean's mind again and he left him a message this time.

Sean stayed at the after-race party for an hour. Sean had a restful night at a hotel in Miami before he flies back home to Auckland. His hotel room had full-sized mirrors on the double-doored closet. Sean looks at himself. Naked.

He raised his hands way up. He stares at his armpits. He squatted outward to check his groin. He then turned to his left and then right, to check the back of his neck. Sean is smiling at himself. Not only because he is super lean, but his symptoms of acanthosis nigricans, due to his pre-diabetes, seem to have disappeared.

Sean sits on his hotel bed to review his list of controllable / uncontrollable / why. He wrote: Uncontrollable: Other people's thoughts and opinions.

At his home office in Auckland, he got a phone call from his GP.
Sean: Yes! Thank you!
Sean hangs up the phone with a big smile on his face.
Sean: Guess what, Peter!
Peter: You got some girl pregnant during the 777 race?
Sean laughs: No! My blood test came back all normal!
Peter: Congratulations, Sean! Should I order pizza now?
Sean throws his eyeglasses case and Peter catches it with his left hand.

Sean's mobile is ringing. It's a +61 number. Sean is certain that it's Yoshi ringing from Australia. Sean was wrong. It's a call from a well-known person from Sydney.

Caller: Hello, Sean. This is Harry Hill from the Truth Podcast in Australia. Do you have a few minutes to talk?
Sean is looking a little puzzled.

Harry: Listen, I came across a footage of your interview at the 777-world challenge and your story about being pre-diabetic. Before we proceed, would you mind telling me what your health condition is now?
Sean: All back to normal, mate.
Harry: That's what I expected. I could have ignored your story; however, I watched a video of you running alongside Ciara, the blind runner from Ireland. I immediately thought there must be a mystery and a story behind this guy. Sean and Harry set a schedule for the podcast interview and recording in Sydney.

Sean's phone rang again. It is Yoshi this time. Sean briefly summarised the outcome of the race. Yoshi sounded he was in a hurry. Sean had scheduled a time with Yoshi and a lawyer in Sydney, so they can meet up about re-opening Yoshi's restaurant.

2 weeks later. Sydney, 8.30am. Sean's interview with Harry went well for the podcast.

That afternoon, Sean, Yoshi and Kevin (the Sydney lawyer) met up at a busy café. Kevin is of Asian background, but he was born in Australia.

Kevin: Summarise to me the situation. Then tell me what outcome you want.

Yoshi had explained the situation written in his journal and the result he wants. He re-wrote these in his journal a few times until it is very clear to him. He read this out loud every night and that's the way he explained it to Kevin. Yoshi expected several questions from Kevin.

Kevin: Let me deal with the NSW FACC authorities. I'll come back to you in a day or two.

Yoshi could tell this lawyer will be brilliant simply because of the way he breathes.

Yoshi: What's your rate, mate?
Kevin: Relax, this is going to be mate's rate.

Yoshi: Thank you. My restaurant has been closed for a while, so I still need to know.
Lawyer whispers the rate to Yoshi.
Yoshi: You're hired.
They shook hands.

The next afternoon:
Kevin with a hint of cigarette smell on his hair: Here's your letter of confirmation to re-open, Mr Hong. My assistant also emailed you a copy forwarded from FACC.
Yoshi: Wow, that's super quick!
Kevin: There is no case to begin with after all. Just off the record, I think some FACC authorities have friends who are threatened by the potential of what you and your restaurant can do. Secondly, they knew they could bully you and so they did! Lastly, there is a dash of unconscious bias against you during the inspection.
Yoshi: A dash?
Kevin: Both you and I look oriental, right? Well, you look half-oriental! In a nano-second, we feel the stereotype judgement even before someone opens their mouth. It's all in the body language and the energy they put out. So, what I do then is I give people a couple of chances, by not being defensive, allowing them to re-arrange the expression on their faces, and to re-phrase their sentences if necessary. Most people revert with a good and apologetic attitude.

That's what happened during my dealing with FACC this morning. The officer knew I wasn't going to budge and will not leave until I had what I needed in my hand. I don't think he even understood the list of your rights I enlisted in front of him.

Yoshi: You're my business and family lawyer from now on. Thank you, Kevin!

Yoshi pre-ordered some fresh produce and beans to be delivered to his restaurant. Yoshi is so grateful to Sean for connecting him with Kevin. So, he is cooking Sean dinner at his restaurant.

Sean and Yoshi exchanged ideas about the future of Mr Hong. How Yoshi wants to expand into other areas of the food industry. How Sean wants to transform his legal practice with some social work.

Sean phone rang. It's Harry Hill the nutritionist podcaster.

Harry: I have a mate in Melbourne who is doing a doco about diabetes. I thought your story will add value to the doco. The film producers will cover your airfare, accommodation, meals and transport. Would you be interested?
Sean: Why not! Given I'm already in Australia.

Sean and Yoshi put on 'On the Road Again', a song from the movie Shrek while they danced to clean the whole kitchen.

Melbourne. Sean is amazed at the sky. Instead of blue, it's more like very light purple. He took Uber from the airport to the city. The filming of the interview is at Degraves Street along the Piccolina Gelateria.

Sean did not prepare for the interview. His objective is to be open and be authentic about his experience. The interviewer was digging into the nitty gritty details and was playing the devil's advocate. Sean thought quietly to himself that this interviewer has forgotten that he is a lawyer. Sean concluded that lifestyle is a big factor. However, he emphasised that connection and being of service to others are vital ingredients for optimum health.

During Sean's interview, he could recognise a girl sitting along the gelateria. Though he is not 100% certain.

After his interview and the girl finished her gelato, he came up to her:

Girl: Sean?
Sean: Oh, my goodness, what a small world! Can I give you a big hug, Alisa?
They hugged as if they were long lost friends.
Sean: I heard you were in the Philippines.

Alisa: Yes. Sorry, this is Amelia. We met in the Philippines. I'm here in Melbourne visiting mum, dad and Rebecca.
Sean: Please to meet you, Amelia.
Alisa looking a bit anxious: I hope Daddy paid all my fees?
Sean: Of course! Your Dad? The best CPA in the world! He wouldn't miss paying bills.
Alisa: I'm so relieved!
Sean: So, how are you going?
Alisa: I've been clean for 6 years, going on 7.
Sean: Good on you, Alisa! I'm so glad for you. How long are you staying here in Melbourne?
Alisa: Longer than I expected. It's not safe for me to be in the Philippines right now.
Sean: Well, let me know how I can help. You know I have lots of contacts.
Sean and Alisa exchanged their revised contact details.

Amelia could feel Alisa's anxiety: Listen, Alisa, don't worry. I don't label anyone about their past. The good thing is that you've been clean for a long time. That says a lot about you. You're a brave person, Alisa.

Chapter 17 – Cutting the Resistance Cord

Amelia has been quietly in pain about her stomach cramps. She looked up the causes and remedies online and that left her confused. Her confusion stem from looking up only the solutions and evidence she wants to believe. Amelia felt she is running out of options. She reached out to Michael, the microbiologist whom she met at the yoga retreat.

Amelia sent Michael a message:
Hi Michael. I'm Amelia, we met at the yoga retreat in Melbourne. How was the conference you attended while you were here? I'm suffering from stomach cramps. I've exhausted all medical assistance. I thought you may be able to help me.

Leaving the scaly skin of the cooked boa constrictor, Michael had eaten all the flesh. Tired and overfed, he fell asleep in his hammock.

That night, he was woken up by a dream about his phone vibrating and the screen brightness level at 100%. Michael managed to go back to sleep but the same dream carried on and on. He thought for a second that the dream is real, so he got up to check his phone. Its battery is flat.

Early next morning, he arranged to go to Manaus, the main city in the Amazonas. There, he spends about 8 hours to charge his equipment battery, to recharge his phone and powerbank. He made phone calls, sent emails and messages in relation to his work.

Michael replied to Amelia:
Hi Amelia, the Melbourne conference went well. I may be able to help you with your stomach issue. Best to video call if you have time in the next few hours.

Amelia: I can FaceTime in 10 minutes.
Michael: Perfect!
On the phone, they both smiled and blushed.

Michael: what are your symptoms?
Amelia: This is embarrassing. I go to the toilet a lot.
Michael: Number 1 or 2?
Amelia: Both. I get cramps on my lower stomach. I'm bloated all the time, and my skin breakouts are getting worst.
Michael: Tell me your food staples.
Amelia: Um, I don't really know. Whatever are high in protein.
Michael: I noticed you weren't eating carbs at the yoga retreat. I have a couple of opinions. These are not advice, okay.
Amelia: Okay.
Michael: Firstly, you could start to include in your meditations that you say thank you to your body. It does a lot for you. Maybe, somewhere in your psyche, you want to punish your body somehow.

Amelia quietly recalls how her ex-boyfriend left her for a girl who is very slim. Amelia said nothing to Michael at this point and gave him a big frown. So, Michael carried on with his second opinion.

Michael: My other opinion is to not focus just on protein. It's highly probable that your body is lacking in other essential nutrients. Your microbes in your stomach are picky so it might help if you feed them a variety of fibre and resistant starch.

Amelia gave Michael a double frown when she heard the word 'starch'. Michael ignored her frown while making sure she is still listening.

Michael then said: In a nutshell, eat the colours of the rainbows from fruits and vegetables, sweet potatoes, plantain or bananas.

Amelia tried not to roll her eyes. A person who meticulously calorie counts would not even look at a banana.

Michael: Do it slowly, start with a quarter cup of anything that is new to you. Got it?

Amelia now squinting her eyes, thinking that Michael is not so attractive anymore.

Amelia: Um, yeah, got it.

Michael: Listen, I must go. I'm going to another conference there in Melbourne maybe in 6 to 8 months. If you want, after you've made some changes, I can do some tests on you. I can analyse the composition of your microbiome.

Amelia tried to hide resistance from her voice and said: Yeah, maybe.

From the Amazonas to the city of Manaus to Fortaleza in Brazil, Martin's Soul ran over 2,300 kms. He now has the overview of the group he is meant to put together. He has been working hard to connect all of them.

Not long after hugging Annie and Ciara at the finish line at Fortaleza, Sean felt a need to pause. Martin sent Sean an image of Yoshi looking lost about his next step for Mr Hong, his restaurant. Yoshi is re-reading his journals and looking lost trying to get a pen.

Sean decided to wait till he gets back at his in-flight bed to message Sean. He forgot and fell asleep.

Martin ran and swum across the Atlantic Ocean to follow Sean to his last race in Miami, Florida. After Sean's interview about his journey on pre-diabetes, Martin sent him another image of Yoshi. Sean left him a message this time.

At Sean's hotel in Miami, while he looks for signs of symptoms of pre-diabetes in front of the mirror. Martin sent Sean a spiritual message:

You have no control over other people's opinions. The only opinion that matters is that of your Soul.

Martin ran 2,320 kms from Miami to Albert Lea, Minnesota. He found Jacob working at the Voyageurs National Park. Martin could feel Jacob's thoughts. Jacob is concerned about his brother not being able to shake off his sadness for a while.

Jacob decided to walk further down the trail along Ash River, just listening to the sound of the water. Martin then gave Jacob the image of Magdalena as they tried to rescue the leatherback turtle. Martin allowed Jacob to focus on Magdalena's t-shirt which had the Mission Blue name and logo beside the right pocket.

During Jacob's lunch break, he Googled Mission Blue in Costa Rica and managed to send an email to their office in the Osa Peninsula. While he was typing his message, he wanted to type that he could not stop thinking about Magdalena. He didn't. He just asked politely if it is possible to pass on the message to Magdalena.

Magdalena received the message from her office while she was in an exchange program in Australia.

Magdalena sent Jacob a message:
Hi Jacob, thank you again for helping us rescue Mr Turtle. He turned out to be a female one and just had babies! I'm currently at an exchange program in Australia. Happy to keep in touch, via FaceTime.

That night, they're on each other's screen.

Jacob: So, how many babies?
Magdalena: Three! That is plenty considering leatherback turtle eggs sometimes have no yolk that would turn into embryo. Wait, I'll show you a short video.
Jacob: Wow!
Jacob felt glad that he was able to help rescue a mother turtle. On the back of his mind, he misses his dad but also have resentment toward him. Jacob and Magdalena chatted for 20 minutes about each other's background.

Jacob: I read that most Costa Rican women are well educated. Where do you get your motivation from?
Magdalena: From experiencing hardship and understanding what challenges my Abuelo and our ancestors have had to endure. I feel I have a responsibility to take the next step to move upwards.
Jacob: That is such a beautiful thing to hear.

Jacob wanted to say how beautiful she is too, but of course he didn't. Jacob explained to her his father's history and his brother's situation. Magdalena: You know what? I will send you some cacao powder that my ancestors have been growing and eating for centuries. I know this sounds hippy, but I've witnessed how this helped a lot of people. It would help your brother feel better. Then perhaps, he can start taking upward steps on his own. The right dose I've been taking is just half a teaspoon early in the morning with my breakfast. I've had no side effects I believe.

Jacob: Thank you, Magdalena.
Magdalena: Well, I got to go. Promise to keep in touch?
Jacob: For sure, 100%. I hope to see you again in person.
Magdalena: Alright then, bye for now.

Jacob went outside to get some fresh air. He could see two small bright lights from a distance, glowing in the dark. It's King David, the leader of the pack. The wolf is looking at Jacob directly, though keeping a distance. Jacob started crying quietly. He started talking to King David, as if he was taking to his father:

Why did you have to leave that way? It's such a lazy and selfish exit! Huh, why? Can you see how sad my brother is? He might do the same as you! Why should I just forgive you?

The wolf turned around and headed for the woods. King David howled for a while. Jacob cried himself to sleep. He still got up early to work. While trailing through the Ash River, he noticed that even the animals and insects are quiet. Perhaps a storm is coming? But there's not a cloud in the sky.
Martin whispers to Jacob:

Your father's trauma is not yours to keep. Cut the cord around your torso and liberate yourself, Jacob. I understand that your wound is very deep. Therefore, it is okay to let go of your cords of trauma a few times.

Jacob closed his eyes and took a deep breath and took a long, slow exhale. Martin whispered to him again:

You are 5% biology, the other 95% of you is physics. That is the physics of light. That is who you are. Listen to that light, Jacob. Be free to shed your light. The heartbreak you feel now is a dot located in a wider blank white canvas world of opportunities.

Martin's last message to Jacob:
Also, follow Magdalena's light. Her strength will lead you.

That night, Martin anticipated to see the Elins. At least one of them. Martin counted in his head the progress he has made so far. More importantly, he wants to know how Alisa is.

Two of the Elins arrived.
Martin: How is Alisa?
Kristian: She is safe is Australia.
Martin: Where is Olav and Aleksander?

Gustav spoke with a sombre tone: They are in Leyte, guiding and protecting Father Joel.

Chapter 18 – Liberate

Eight months before Alisa flew to Melbourne, Alisa sat down in the mayor's office. She spotted a couple of cameras on the corners of the ceiling. The mayor, looking quite handsome in his mid-50's, sat down on his high-back black leather chair.

Mayor: I believe you would like to discuss a situation in Lake Bito. How can I help you, Iha (young woman)?

Alisa: Our black sand is being dug up from Lake Bito. I'm concerned about the lake becoming fragile, not just for us but also for all the other creatures within and around the lake. I'm also worried about the livelihood of our fishermen. I would ask you to visit the lake at dawn so you could see what it looks like. Butas-butas po ang lake (the lake is full of holes).

Mayor: Thank you for this important information, Alisa. No one has the permission to dig or do any business activity in and around Lake Bito. The only exception is that the fishermen are allowed to fish limited amount of tilapia to sell only within the community. Leave it with me, I will arrange for one of the councillors to investigate.

Alisa. Salamat po, mayor. I will call you in two weeks for any update.
Mayor: Of course, Alisa.

The guards guided Alisa out of the office and out to the main door of the municipio.

Every fortnight, Alisa would call and leave a message to the mayor's voicemail. She awaits a reply. Alisa has gone back to the lake and the digging carries on.

Alisa and Father Joel then founded The Holy Sand Foundation. Its main objective is to protect the lake. Within 7 months, many members of the community joined the Foundation, which includes the rich, poor, young, old and many fishermen. Pressure is building up throughout the whole town as members of the Foundation record the digging during dawn. One morning, Alisa, Father Joel, and at least 150 members of the Foundation formed a barricade to stop the digging.

Father Eddie organised for some members of the media to attend the activity at Lake Bito.

The mayor then put a moratorium on the digging of the lake.
After a week, Alisa, Father Joel and Father Eddie started receiving letters by mail. The letters contain death threats. Despite their report to the police, the letters continued. Father Joel convinced Alisa to move to Australia for her own safety.

In the meantime, Martin, while in conversation with the Elins at Albert Lea, Minnesota:

Martin: What is going on in the Philippines?
Kristian: There have been disruptions in Lake Bito, but it is starting to settle down now.
Martin: How is Father Joel?
Gustav: He is safe inside the retirement village. Though his health is taking a downturn.
Martin: I want to see Alisa.

Kristian and Gustav grabbed Martin's arms, and they flew to Melbourne where Alisa is.

Kristian: Martin, your objective today is to convince Alisa to come home to look after Father Joel.
Martin: But she would not be safe there!
Gustav: We will all guide and protect her.

Martin watched Alisa sleep and then he put her white rosary around her wrist. Alisa was dreaming during sleep that she is looking after Father Joel.

Alisa woke up and washed up in the bathroom. She put her thick black hair in a high bun, noticing the rosary in her wrist. Standing behind Alisa, Martin held her tight. Alisa exhaled and felt Martin's warmth all over her back and neck.

Alisa's phone rang. It's Father Eddie. He explained to Alisa that Father Joel went for a walk early this morning but has not returned late this evening.

Alisa explained the situation to her father. She asked him to drive him to Watergardens Shopping Mall to pick up the walking shoes she ordered online for Father Joel.

While in the SUV:
Alisa: Father Joel must have wandered in his own.
Carlo: I'm sure they will find him soon.

Alisa went to Rebel Sports shop to get the shoes. While Carlo waits in the car, he noticed a couple of people trying to approach strangers in the carpark. As Alisa comes back approaching her father's car, the two individuals rushed to Alisa. Carlo then got out of his car and abruptly told the two individuals to leave her daughter alone.

Alisa: Thank you, Daddy. Never again, Daddy. I would not ruin my life or yours again. They hugged each other.

In the meantime. Martin is trying to find out from the Elins the whereabouts of Father Joel.

Martin would not let Alisa out of his sight. As usual, he watched her sleep.

While Carlo drops off Alisa at the airport:
Alisa: I'm sorry, Daddy. I'm not who you expected me to be.
Carlo: No need to apologise, anak (child). My dreams are not your dreams. I get it now. To love is to liberate. You make me proud of how brave you have become.
Alisa: I love you, Daddy.

Carlo: I love you too, anak.

Alisa and Martin arrived at the retirement village. Father Joel is still missing. The manager of the retirement village has already made reports to the police. Alisa went out to where she used to take Father Joel for a walk. No trace of him there.

Then, Alisa noticed 3 trees around the edge of Lake Bito. The leaves on the 3 trees are unusually white which stood out among the green leaves from all the other trees. Alisa walked towards the trees to satisfy her curiosity. She touched the leaves, they're softer, with a hint of vanilla aroma. The trees had some unusual flowers which looks like cattleya. Then, Alisa noticed something moved along the trunk of one of the white trees further along.

A hand with white sleeves touched the dried leaves on the ground. Alisa though that it is Father Joel. It is him, sitting with his back against the tree.

Alisa: Father Joel! I'm home!

Alisa rushed to Father Joel. He didn't move. Then, he fell on the ground. Alisa checked his pulse. Alisa sobbed like a child. Father Joel is gone.

Martin watched Alisa from a distance as he cries. Martin didn't know he could do such a thing; he immediately created a big invisible bubble-like dome surrounding Alisa to protect her.

Chapter 19 – A Group of Active Hope

Sean has had a tremendously busy week. As a barrister, he became influential towards some of his clients to change a few of their bad habits. Particularly, a young man in his early 20s. Sean showed him how to create and regularly review and read outload his written goals and reasons in the Controllable/Uncontrollable/Why A3 sheet.

Finally, Sean gets a day off. He woke up itching to go for a run. He wanted to run somewhere else. He drove over the Auckland Harbour Bridge, without a plan, he ended up in Browns Bay.

Sean found the beach and started running along the rocky shore and coastal path. He run toward Rothesay Bay, to Mairangi Bay, along the Milford shops and into Takapuna Beach. He started feeling hungry. He feels that Browns Bay has a more community feel so he decided to run all the way back. He looked up to the clouds as if he is thanking the heavens. During his run, he feels clarity and peace.

Catching his breath, he is very hungry. He walked along Clyde Road and hidden along another street, he found 'Land & Monkeys' formerly known as 'La Tropezienne', a French bakery and café. Sean stood at the back and stared undecidedly at the croquembouche, the mille feuille, éclair, Paris-brest, galette, macaron, choux au craquelin, brioche tarte, clafoutis, palmier, florentine, mont blanc, opera cake, canelé, croissant, dark chocolate souffle, chocolate religieuse.

A customer at the counter gladly said to the teller: I can't believe everything here is plant-based.

Five steps to his right, there's sandwiches: seitan caesar bun, vegan brie on walnut, seitan celery triangle, silky tofu n'egg roll and lox roll.

He asked a waitress if he could use the toilet first. Sean went through a double swing door and a small hallway, the baking area to his left. He noticed the big paper sacks of organic flour on his right.

He opened the toilet door and burst out laughing. The whole toilet room was filled with seashells, beach and sea creature ornaments. All four walls and the ceiling are filled with them. The toilet seat is see-through aqua. He flicked the light switched and laughed again. It lit light blue like the ocean. As Sean did his business, he decided he would treat himself with food today.

Sitting in one corner of the café, next to a black and white large photograph of a French woman kissing a man in the train station in the 1950s, Sean smiles as he drinks his re-fillable café-filtre. He devours his vegan sandwich, scrambled chickpea n'eggs on croissant with mushroom and spinach on the side, Florentine and religieuse. Sean licks his fingers as he picks up the last crumb.

Sean's phone rang.

Sean: Hello, you're speaking with Sean.
Caller: Hi Sean, this is Alisa calling from the Philippines. Is it convenient for you to talk now? I need your help.
Sean: Yes, of course, Alisa. Isn't it quite early over there?
Alisa: I'm sorry to call you so early.
Sean: It's fine. I've been awake for 3 hours. Are you okay? How can I help?
Alisa: I'm not in trouble. Though I'm feeling unsafe and terribly lost. I called you coz I needed to talk to someone out of my main circle.
Sean: Well, it's your lucky day! Shoot, Alisa, I'm here to listen.
Alisa: Thank you, Sean.

There's another call coming through Sean's phone. Sean accidentally added the call to his conversation with Alisa.

Sean: Hello. This is Sean.
Caller. Sean, my man! It's Yoshi!
Sean: Hello, Yoshi! Sorry, mate, I'm on another call.

Alisa: Oh, it's okay.

Alisa had a call coming through. It's Amelia.
Amelia: Hey Alisa, I've been worried about you.

Alisa added Amelia to the call. Amelia had a call from Michael. She added him to the conversation too. Magdalena called Amelia and Jacob called Magdalena.

All seven individuals are now connected digitally, strangers among another, after chatting for almost 3 hours, laughing, exchanging their hopes and dreams, they've somehow inspired one another.

Alisa: thank you Sean and everyone. I feel like I have some direction now. I've isolated myself for the last three months. I think I'm ready to be out again.

Martin stood from a distance from Alisa. He vanished the bubble dome surrounding her.

Alisa decided to put away the photos of Father Joel's funeral. She noticed one thing. Everyone from the retirement village was at the funeral except for one person.

Alisa: Father Eddie, how come Jenny wasn't at the funeral?
Father Eddie: She was sick I believe.
Alisa: I don't think I've seen her around.
Father Eddie: I think she resigned, recently.
Alisa: Okay.

Martin run to find out where Jenny is. Jenny is at home supervising the building of the second floor of her mother's house. When the builders left, she started cleaning her brand-new car. Then she proceeded to look after her elderly mother.

Martin called upon the Elins.
Martin: What was the cause of Father Joel's death.
Kristian: Pneumonia.

Martin: I'm following Jenny, a former caretaker of Father Joel. I think something else went on.
Gustav: Martin, you do know that despite us (the Elins) being able to fly, we can only be at one place at a time?
Martin: I see.
Aleksander: Martin, your mission is to get a group of people together.
Martin: I have.
Olav: Thank you, Martin. What is their next step?
Martin: Will you guide me?

Chapter 20 – Swallowed by Rain

Michael, while in Manaus, travelled back in a hurry to where his mother is. He heard some news about gun shots towards a Yanomami tribe by illegal goldminers. The local television news showed Yanomami children tied up against some posts inside their 'yano'. Michael is super anxious because he is required to go back to the US for work in a few weeks.

Marima's tribe is safe. Meeting was held among the leaders (shamans) and the elderly. The tribe has done everything they could to prepare in case an attack does eventuate.

That night, it's bucketing down with rain. Rainfall that none of the Yanomami elders has ever seen before. The water in the river beside the shabonos is flowing wild.

By 4am, water started to flow through the shabonos. Everyone in the village knew what to do, including young children. Each member took some tools. They gathered and walked uphill away from the shabonos.

Michael: Where are we going?
Shaman: Look at the flow of the river, Michael.
Micheal: I'm not sure if it's going south.
Shaman: In the Amazon basin, water only flows in one direction – downhill. So, we are going in the opposite direction of the flow of the river. We know another Yanomami tribe up the hill.

Michael was cautiously protecting his mother on the way to the other village. The other tribe was welcoming and Marima's tribe was told they could stay as long as they need to.

The following afternoon, Marima announced to the tribe that the miners have temporarily stopped their work because the heavy rainfall has swallowed up all their trucks and machines. "Not a trace of any of them!" Marima yelled as she raised both her hands up. She asked each tribe member to take out their black bands made from monkey tails, off their arms. Each member put it in the woven bucket in the middle of the yano. They use these black arm bands as part of their dance to summon the spirit xapiripe and ask for rain. The shamans inhaled yakoana powder to summon the spirits to protect them from violence.

Marima introduced Michael to the oldest member of the tribe. Nobody knows exactly how old she is. Marima thinks she would be at least 100 years old. The woman, still standing tall, laughed hysterically when Marima told her that Michael takes samples of Yanomami urine and stool to study for the western world. Michael started laughing along with them and he whispers to himself, "Yeah, I know, this modern world has come to this - studying shit!" The woman nodded and hugged Michael. Michael politely asked her if he could take samples of her urine and stool. That afternoon, the elderly woman did her business, and Michael took care of the rest.

That night, Michael arranged for some of the samples to be transported to Monash University in Melbourne, Australia. This forms part of his work in microbiology. The objective is to proceed with the idea of faecal transplant to patients who suffer from chronic pain. Monash University is also studying patients with IBS with the use self-hypnosis. This hypnosis method is making positive changes to about 20% of the patients.

The next day, Michael messaged Amelia to tell her about the two possible solutions for her IBS. Michael suggested that she does both. Self-hypnosis first with the guide of the university and then do the faecal transplant. Michael especially requested from the staff of the university to transplant the samples from the 100-year-old Yanomami woman to Amelia.

Michael told Amelia that this procedure has been completed randomly at US hospitals. The unconfirmed news from hospitals is that the benefits of the transplant seem to work for several weeks for most patients. The cramps would go away as soon as the day after of the transplant. However, when the patients go back to their normal diets, the cramps or chronic pain comes back after about a month. It seems, that the 'good' microbes are washed out. So, the idea is to get the patients to keep feeding the microbes with fibre and resistant starch. Amelia sighed as soon as she heard that word 'starch' again.

Six months later, Amelia volunteered to pick up Michael from the Tullamarine Airport. Michael did not recognise Amelia.
Amelia: Hey, Michael. I'm here!
Michael: Amelia?
Amelia: Yeah, thanks to you, I feel awesomely good and energetic.
Michael: So, it worked!
Amelia: I can't wait to hear about this amazing 100-year-old woman.

Amelia and Michael laughed and talked non-stop in the car. Amelia dropped him off at his hotel.

Michael: Do you want to come in for herbal tea?
Amelia: Herbal tea?
Michael: Yeah! We don't want to dilute your microbes with alcohol!

It's 11pm and there's a big dark cloud looming.

Michael: Rain seems to follow me wherever I go!

Amelia laughed as she gets ready to leave. Michael grabs her waist and gently moved her against the hallway wall, getting ready to kiss her.

Chapter 21 – The Chef that Could Cure

The sound of pots and pans, the hiss of the gas burner, the chefs calling out the name of the dishes, are getting louder and faster. Mr Hong just received another Michelin star.

In the last 8 months since Mr Hong re-opened, word of mouth has spread about Yoshi's menu. His dishes with his Plant-Based (PB) cheese creations have become a massive hit. In addition to the desert selection, Mr Hong has a cheese board presenting the 4 plant-based cheese (camembert, sharp blue, smoked, truffle) along with Mr Hong's house-made squares of focaccia, crackers, quandong and finger lime marmalade and walnuts from Wellwood Organic Orchard. The bigger hit is one of the entrees in the menu – baked plant-based camembert with a drizzle of manuka vegan honey, garnished with thyme purple flowers, served with warm focaccia.

Regular customers started to ask if they could purchase some cheese to take home. Yoshi hired 2 more chefs and 2 more waiting staff to keep up with the growth of customer bookings. He also hired a duty manager so he could concentrate on making his plant-based cheese creations. Yoshi started to make wheels of cheese about 7 centimetres in diameter. Yoshi delegated Alan to organise a simple and sustainable packaging for the plant-based cheese wheels.

After two weeks, a flat and wide display fridge is being installed inside Mr Hong's. Yoshi strategically located the display fridge along the walkway just before the counter area. The plant-based wheels of cheese are displayed neatly with each wheel lined up resting on a small wooden stand. When Mr Hong's staff slowly open the small door of the fridge, customers can smell the cheese, and some customers hinted that it reminded them of Paris.

Yoshi added in his journal:

The microbes from the rejuvelac that I use for the cheese must be working wonders in my customers' stomach. Perhaps they're starting to feel better too.

A woman in her 40s did a post on TikTok and Instagram showing her before and after photo. In her post she is saying that she lost weight and feels more energetic due to her regular running. She then emphasised that she's a regular at Mr Hong's and that she's been feeling amazing since she started eating Mr Hong's cheeses. In her 40s, this woman is voluptuous and drop dead gorgeous. Her followers can see how much weight she dropped in six months. She has 2 million followers around the world, 400 odd thousand are from Sydney. And so, her post went viral.

The queue outside Mr Hong's is about 300 metres long the following weekend. Yoshi called in his parents to take the customers details in the queue for a pre-order. Alan, Yoshi's dishy, then did a post in Instagram to let customers know that the cheese has sold out and asked them to send a message or an email to pre-order.

Monday, Mr Hong is closed for business. While Yoshi is taking in his stock and produce delivery, a man approached him, handed him his business card and told Yoshi that he is a capital venture investor. Yoshi told him that he will call him around 4pm.

Yoshi and the man, named Jim, had a drink at a nearby bar. Though Jim seems genuine to Yoshi, he told Jim that he will think about his proposal.

Yoshi contacted Sean to let him know about Jim's idea to invest in his plant-based cheese creations. Sean told Yoshi to give him a couple of days as Sean is attending to a family matter.

Sean haven't seen his mother for 12 years. He received a call from his Auntie yesterday to let him know that his mother needs help.

Sean: I'm not giving her any more money. She will just gamble it away.

Auntie: Your mother did counselling for the last 8 years and she's been clean for the last 5 years.

Sean: So, what does she want now?

Auntie: She can no longer manage her home. The 2-storey home is too big for her and she's becoming frail.
Sean: I'll see if I can have some time off.

Sean put the thought of seeing her mother aside again.

Sean called Kevin. Sean asked him if he could investigate Jim, the investor. Kevin called Sean the next day to confirm that Jim is a legitimate investor. In fact, he is a big fish in the investment start-up space in Australia.

Harry Hill, the nutritionist and podcaster also heard about the news on Yoshi's creations and restaurant. He organised to meet with Yoshi at the restaurant. Harry politely asked Yoshi if he could see the blood test results of Yoshi's parents before and a few months after they've been eating the plant-based cheese.

Yoshi's parents agreed to show the results to Harry at their home. Harry is impressed. Though he emphasised that he would need to consider other factors or any other changes which Yoshi's parents did during that same period. Harry is also concerned about the 2 flavours which contains coconut oil. Though he noted that they are minimal. He mentioned to Yoshi that it may not be suitable for people with cardiovascular issues or people with high bad cholesterol.

Somehow, Jim got hold of Harry Hill over the telephone. Jim wanted to clarify some facts. Harry informed him that he would rather have Yoshi's plant-based cheese than any other plant-based cheese available in Australia, or any dairy cheese for that matter. Harry told Jim that Yoshi's creations are nutritionally sound because most of the ingredients are from wholefood and that they are very delicious.

Harry: The only thing is that 2 of his flavours have coconut oil, which I will be staying away from, as my family have history of cardiovascular disease.

Harry continues his explanation to Jim:
Imagine! If so many people are switching to plant-based cheese, that would free-up so much land in Australia. A big chunk of farmland is used to produce dairy products. I understand that the dairy industry and their workers would have a rock up. But that is already happening in the US where dairy companies as going bankrupt. The dairy workers can easily be trained to work for the plant-based industry instead.

The next day, Yoshi called Sean.
Sean: Yoshi, I think you're onto something big here. Jim is legit. As a matter of fact, Kevin said he's a big fish!
Yoshi: Okay, I don't know how these things work. Can you and Kevin help me?
Sean: How firm is your handshake, Yoshi? Once we start the process, there's no turning back.
Yoshi: Sure, mate. I'll give Kevin a call to see if we can have Mr Hong and the cheese partnership as two separate ownerships.
Sean: That would be what Kevin will do first. But be quick at making decisions, mate. You want to take the opportunity while the iron is hot!

Kevin and his team at his law firm did not waste any time at all. In just two weeks, the legal documents were reviewed, approved and are ready for signing.

Jim called Kevin the night before the meeting.
Jim: We need to make this bigger, Kevin.
Kevin: In relation to what, Jim?
Jim: I'm putting in 40 million and I don't think it will be enough to really scale.
Kevin: Oh, don't be in such a hurry, Jim. That will be the next step.
Jim: Oh, you too, can see how big this can go!
Kevin: Of course, mate! We would also have the dairy industry CEOs and their lawyers, guns blazing on our back!
Jim: Exciting times, mate! See you tomorrow.

Kevin rang Yoshi to ensure he is all set for the meeting.
Kevin: See you at 9am tomorrow, Yoshi!
Yoshi: Yeah, mate! I even have my suit ironed up and ready.

9am. Kevin, Jim and his lawyer are in the boardroom. Kevin rang Yoshi and left a message.

Kevin left a few more messages. He rang the restaurant, he's not there. The staff called him too but no luck. Alan called Yoshi's family, but they did not answer either.

Alan called Kevin and said that this is not like Yoshi at all. He would at least leave a message if he could not make it. Alan volunteered to go to Yoshi's house.

Alan then called Kevin: No trace of Yoshi I'm sorry. It's really strange that there's no one at home but both front and back doors are wide open, and Yoshi's car and his parents' car are still here.

Chapter 22 – Listen Carefully

Martin went back to Jenny's home, Father Joel's former caretaker. This time, Martin went early in the morning. Martin found Jenny soaking mushrooms in soap and water while she wore gloves and facemask. Jenny then put the wet mushrooms in a plastic bag, drove over to the next town and parked her car in a quiet street. Walked for 20 minutes and put the bag in a big bin at the back of a big restaurant.

Martin called the Elins and advised them that Jenny may have played a role in Father Joel's death. The Elins held hands with Martin, rewinding back events that have happened. Martin could see the events very clearly as if they were happening at that moment.

Jenny used to feed Father Joel champorado for breakfast most mornings. But before she served it, she would put fried salty dried fish pieces on it. This is the usual way most Filipinos would eat champorado. But Jenny would put a separate type of fish for Father Joel which she discretely takes from her bag in the kitchen.

Jenny has been using mushrooms instead for Father Joel. Jenny prepared it at home in a makeshift kitchen in her backyard. She sliced the mushroom thinly and soaks them in fish sauce and soy sauce. The mushroom gave the look, smell and taste similar to that of fried salty dried fish.

Martin and the Elins then went to the restaurant to try and retrieve the mushroom in the bin. The mushroom is Amanita Pseudo Porphyria, also known as false death cap. It has 2-amino-4 and 5 hexadecenoic acid. A poisonous mushroom that grows around Asia.

Martin: How could the 4 of you not know what was happening?

Kristian: Martin, there is a lot happening in this little Earth of ours! We could not be in all places at once!

Gustav: Situations like these happens when humans are indecisive, when humans go where it's comfortable and safe, when they are not focused on their purpose.

Martin: What! Are you guys blaming Alisa for this?
Martin shakes his head as he sits down on the ground.

Olav: The dark spirits are at work, Martin; we must fight them too.
Aleksander: This is why it's imperative that we must work closely together. Martin, we need to be super focused, and we need to work faster. Our timeline is becoming very tight. Your group need to make things happen a lot faster. Otherwise, we will have to find and work with another group.

Martin stood up and sighs: Okay, I would need your guidance.

Kristian: Listen carefully as we communicate through your Soul, Martin. Do not deviate from what we ask you to do. Listen and do.

Martin went to Alisa and whispered to her: *Jenny.* Alisa went to find Jenny at her home. From a distance, Alisa saw one of the mayor's security guards come out of Jenny's front door.

Alisa: This is really strange. Are they lovers? How could she afford to put a second floor on their house and a new car.

As far as Alisa knows, Jenny has not taken up a new job.

While Alisa is sleeping, Martin gave her the details of what happened to Father Joel through her dream. Alisa woke up full of sweat and said, 'Oh, Dios ko!'

The next morning, Alisa advised the managers at the resthome, and they then reported the events to the police. The police did investigate. They could not open a case as they could not find any proof.

In her bathroom, Alisa stared at her reflection in the mirror. Martin stood next to her. They are both nostalgic about their current situation. Alisa unaware that another Soul is right next to her.

They both knew. Alisa is putting her life on the line to protect Lake Bito. Alisa decided not to tell her parents so they would not worry.

Martin is at a loss – between protecting Alisa and pushing her to take action to save Lake Bito. All he is sure about is that he does not want to go to the higher world.

Martin whispered *Call Sean* to Alisa. Then, he whispered *Magdalena.*

Alisa rang Sean and explained to him what had happened.

Sean: You did everything you could for Father Joel, Alisa.
Alisa. Thank you, Sean. I don't know what else I could do for Lake Bito. The Foundation has done all it could. I'm not sure if the moratorium has been lifted. The digging and sand sucking has started again.

Sean: Let me contact my circle and I will find an environmental lawyer to contact you. Alisa also called Magdalena and asked her about the process of applying for Lake Bito along with Leyte Gulf to become a Hope Spot with Mission Blue.

Chapter 23 – I am so Tired. Please Heal Me.

Lilly, Jacob's sister is banging her head gently as she stood facing the outside bathroom wall. She really needs to pee. Her brother, Bryan has been taking a bath for the last hour. Lilly is concerned that Bryan is not responding to her at all.

There is no one else at home so Lilly went to the next-door neighbour. The neighbour used some tools to unlock the bathroom door. The neighbour quickly went in front of Lilly blocking the view inside the bathroom. He quickly closed the door and took Lilly to another room. He rang another neighbour to look after her in the meantime.

Bryan is unconscious. He slit his wrist vertically from his palm. His blood made the water pink. He is still breathing. The ambulance took Bryan to the hospital. Jacob and his mother have been interchangeably visiting him at the hospital for two weeks. Bryan is then transferred to a recovery facility.

Jacob rang Magdalena to tell her what happened. It turns out Bryan had run out of cacao powder two months ago and never asked for more. He has been quietly suffering from depression again.

Jacob: I don't know why I didn't pick up on this. I really thought he was feeling better.
Magdalena: Some things you just cannot know.

Martin whispered to Jacob: *Ask Magdalena if Bryan can go to Costa Rica to participate in the growing and harvesting of cacao.*

One month later, Bryan's trip to Costa Rica has been organised. Though still looking sad at the airport, there's a hint of excitement on his face as he waved bye at the departures area.

Magdalena asked her Abuelo, Pablo, to make arrangements for Bryan to stay and work with the Bribri tribe at the Kallari Cacao Farm which is led by Don Morales.

Bryan was welcomed with a ceremony, which he thought was just some kind of a rain dance. It turned out to be a lot more than that.

Don Morales is already aware of Bryan's health. He arranged with a few tribe members to gather and start a chant ceremony for Bryan.

Bryan was led to the middle and the tribe members encircled him and started chanting with rasp drums and rascas (scrapers). Bryan found the chant very soothing. It was a chant to channel Ix Chel. Ix Chel, although a god for fertility, she is also a goddess of medicine.

The tribe then led Bryan to the tallest cacao tree which is about 12 metres tall. The tribe chanted to channel Chaac, the god of rain and patron of agriculture. The ceremony was followed by a feast.

Once Bryan was settled in his small makeshift room within the farm, he walked toward the tallest cacao tree. He hugged it as if he was a child being held by his mother. Bryan said to the tree: *I am tired. I am really tired. Please heal me.*

Bryan wandered for a few minutes, and he noticed how there were so many different varieties of plants, shrubs and other trees that surround the cacao trees. There were some yucas, coffee bushes, mahogany, coconut palm and banana trees.

Bryan spotted some cacao pods that look maroon from a distance but more like deep purple as he got closer. He squints his eyes and smiles at the same time. He looked up to the sky, wanting to pinch himself and said to himself: Wow! Am I really somewhere else? He noticed the more earthy smell of the soil opposed to the dusty smell of the soil in Minnesota.

On his way back to his room, he noticed some maize growing alongside some beans and pumpkin on the ground. Bryan was curious so he peeked through one of the maize cobs. He was expecting to see cream or yellow-coloured kernels. He laughed. Instead, they were, bright yellow, purple, blue, red, lilac and white – all in one cob.

Bryan slept in his room with mosquito netting. His sleep was unsettled because the mozzies were bussing outside the net.

The next morning, Don Morales welcomed Bryan with three different kinds of cacao pods (Theobroma Cacao Cultevars).

One with seeds that are sweet and usually used during festivals. It's the fruity, floral and nutty variety, usually coloured kind of red and purple and it is called the Trinitario variety.

The second variety is called Criollo. A green yellowy coloured pod with seeds that are mildly acidic and rarely bitter. The farm does not have many of this variety as it is less resistant to disease.

The third variety, Forastero is coloured light brown, with seeds that are bitter. Forastero cacaos are used for healing of illness.

The tribe members handed Bryan a medium-sized machete. The group walked to the cacao forests. They showed him how to spot the ones that are ripe and how to cut the cacao fruits pods from the trees. They also asked him to pick up the pods that have fallen on the ground. A couple of men were using a long wooden stick with a curved knife at the end to get the pods that are up high. Bryan was handed a big woven basket to put the pods in.

Late in the afternoon, the tribe gathered in one area of the farm, and they showed Bryan how to cut open the pods and put the seeds in the allocated clean baskets. One of the leaders explained to Bryan that the farm is part of the chakras, a group that work to protect their culture and their environment.

Martin swam and run to the farm and led Bryan to a small book about cacao. Bryan is physically tired but found the book interesting, so he read the book each night. Bryan learned that cacao has theobromine, which is similar to caffeine, however instead of it giving some people palpitations, cacao tends to relax the heart.

He learned that cacao has phenethylamine, which could help lift depression. That cacao has flavonoids that could lower blood pressure and could act as a blood thinner to avoid blood clots.

More importantly, he reads the precautions that cacao could lead to negative outcomes if large doses are taken. That cacao has anandamide, a chemical that similar to the make-up of THC giving individuals the feeling of euphoria. If taken in large doses and/or too late in the day, this could lead to sleepless nights and eventually lead to anxiety.

Bryan told himself: *Aha! The dose AND the timing are the key!*

Bryan fell in deep sleep after reading the book. Martin stood next to Bryan's bed and gave him the following dream:

A group of people from varied ethnicities and racial backgrounds are all doing a meditation. The dream focused on the mat they are sitting on, with different vibrant colours interwoven beside each other making the Matt very durable [4].

Bryan woke up. Sitting up on his bed at 4am. Thinking to himself: *That is the answer! No more separation. We all will have to be interwoven to make this world a better place. Just like the cacao trees surrounded by other plants, shrubs and native trees, they work in harmony all mix in in one place.*

The next day, the group was focusing on taking as many seeds as possible out of the pods. Bryan is physically tired, but he internally feels happy and peaceful. Martin whispered to him:

The cacao trees are exchanging microbes back and forth with the other trees through their roots. They also emit chemicals when pests are around to protect each other. That cacao trees have been trying to show humanity for centuries that biodiversity is the key to growth and evolution. That uniformity and sameness only breaths stagnant energy. Eventually, this stagnant energy becomes poisonous.

While Bryan enjoys the smell of fresh cacao seeds, Martin whispered to him that the cacao trees have been around for so long, so they have watched many civilisations rise and fall. That the trees feel our happiness and sorrows. One of the tribesmen explained to Bryan that they can see the magnetic field coming directly from the cacao trees which channels between the other world and the trees.

Bryan then felt a spurt of tingle that travelled from his tailbone, through his spine and onto the back of his neck. Bryan closed his eyes and whispered to himself: The cacao trees now call on us to help heal ourselves and our Earth.

Bryan rang his brother Jacob about his visions. Jacob rang Magdalena so she could also join their conversation. Bryan spoke with his sister Lilly to give her an update.

The next morning, Bryan and the men are getting ready to lay the beans flat on big mats to allow them to ferment and dry.

One of the tribesmen approached Bryan. This man looks rather angry. He is holding a machete and started talking to Bryan in an abrupt manner. Bryan is of course looking upset and not understanding a word of what this man is saying. One of the leaders got up. He was trying to explain to Bryan that everyone here is trying to help you heal. But you cannot heal with the food and the environment alone. You must release the trauma that you have been holding inside you since you arrived here.

Bryan: Oh, you are right. Muchos Gracias. Por Favor, show me how I can release this trauma I have inside of me since I was little.

Tribe leader: Pray, meditate and go for walks in nature early in the morning.
Bryan: Si, Señor.
Don Morales: We will also teach you to chant to Ix Chel.

Don Morales allocated two tribesmen to teach Bryan the chant. Bryan had the chants down packed after 5 weeks. Bryan's eyes are looking brighter, and he hasn't been concerned about his cancer for a single moment.

At 4am, Bryan got up to meditate beside the cacao trees. While he sat down quietly on the ground, he received some telepathic messages from Chaac, the patron of agriculture:

Mother Nature wants you to give back. Make heart-led decisions. You need a diverse group of friends to help you give back to Mother Nature. If humans do not co-operate with each other and evolve, humanity is headed to catastrophe. Our Earth itself is angry about mining, about the soil turning into dust, about the ocean slowly cooking. Chanting to the water, land and spirits is no longer sufficient. So much damage has been done.

Shadowing the Chaac, is the Soul of Martin. Martin is hard at work, getting the group to all connect again.

Martin whispered to Bryan to call Jacob and asked him to go on top of the hill to get better reception. Jacob dialled in Magdalena to join in. She then got Michael to join the call.

Bryan asked them if he could set up a group chat for them. All said yes.

Michael said: You might as well include the others: Alisa, Amelia, Sean and Yoshi. Hey Bryan, what should we name the group.
Bryan shrugs his shoulder: I don't know. Everyone seems to be talking from their inner self. You know, like they're from their inner core or their Soul.

Michael chuckles: Like a bunch of Soul hippies?

Martin is laughing translucently in the background. Martin is watching Bryan standing on a hill. A hill is called 'haugen' in Norwegian. Or a group or a pile could also mean 'haugen'. Martin whispered it to Jacob.

Jacob: What about Haugen Soul?

Martin laughs again and whispered jokingly to Jacob: No, you drongo! The other way around.
Magdalena: Soulhaugen.
Michael: You know what, that sounds really good, I like it! Let me just check Uncle Google in case it means something rude in another language. Oh! What a fluke! In Norwegian, it means 'A pile of Souls.'

Two months later, a buzzing sound of a black drone goes passed above some land. Amelia, Jacob, Bryan, Michael and Magdalena are planting seedlings and cacao seeds in round pockets of soil by hand. This time, they are in the Far North Queensland. Amelia and Michael both learned how to use the drone to also help the team plant more seeds, to assess weather patterns and factors that may affect the microbiome of the soil.

Martin has done a lot of reading and observing many communities and has been closely liaising with the Elins. Some natives in the Amazon are gaining wins to protect their forests, through other groups that the Elins are working with.

One of Soulhaugen's mission now is to grow as many cacao trees and varieties of Australian native trees as possible in the far North of Queensland to combat the significant deforestation in that area.

While planting, Michael is explaining to Bryan that our gut microbes does not like food grown with pesticides and synthetic fertilizers.

Bryan: Yes, we will have to grow these trees organically. I've never seen the Bribri tribe use any of that stuff.

A truck arrived. The driver then unloads young banana plants, yuca roots, mahogany plants, Aboriginal native plants, fruit trees and a variety of vegetable seedlings. Michael and Amelia took out their drawn-up plan so they know how each variety will surround the cacao trees.

Martin had joined them in the background. His plan is to see Yoshi in Sydney, then see Sean in New Zealand. Instead, he started running north towards the Philippines to see how Alisa is.

Chapter 24 – Love is the Only Reality

Two of the Elins stopped Martin on the way to the Philippines.

Kristian: We need you to stick to our plan, Martin.

Gustav: See Yoshi and Sean to help them with their mission, and then you can proceed to assist Alisa.

Martin: I know, I know. I have a feeling something is going wrong in Leyte.

Kristian: We understand your concern. While you assist Yoshi and Sean, we are flying back to Leyte.

Martin: By the way, can I ask you, this is a little side tracked, but I need to know. What does it mean to be in love in your world?

Kristian: Oneself is in love with the whole.

Gustav: He means, in our world, you are not in love with a particular person. Firstly, you yourself is deserving of your love and affection. Only then, you could love your whole world, umm, muti-verse, for that matter.

Kristian: Once you love your Soul, you will soon realise that the only reality is love.

Martin: Thanks. I think it will take me some time for that wisdom to sink in.

Martin ran to Sydney to find Yoshi. Martin found him deep in their backyard. Martin walked carefully in steep downhill as he watched Yoshi try to comfort his grandfather, Kiyoshi, who slipped and injured his back and could not get up.

Yoshi: Grandpa, we keep telling you not to wear those thongs (flip flops) anymore! They are so worn out and has no grip. While trying to rescue his grandpa, Yoshi accidentally dropped his mobile phone, and it hit a rock. His phone smashed into pieces.

That night, Yoshi bought a new phone and scheduled another meeting with Kevin and Jim.

Martin then went to Auckland, New Zealand to see Sean. He directed Sean to get in touch with CIEL (Centre for International Environmental Law). The next day, Sean has got CIEL to draft a brief so that Alisa could then get it delivered and serve to DENR (Department of Environment and Natural Resources). Sean ensured that a Senior Attorney is assigned to the case of protecting Lake Bito.

The Elins sent Martin a message that Alisa is busy showing the volunteer staff from Mission Blue the situation at Lake Bito.

Martin decided to run to 90-mile beach and soaked himself there for a couple of hours, pondering about what the Elins said about love.

Alisa was feeling tired by late afternoon. She went to bed early. She got her clothes ready for the next day to go to Sunday mass. She hasn't been for a while.

At the church, Alisa could see Jenny from a distance. After the mass, Alisa came up to Jenny and asked her how she is. Alisa then asked her why she wasn't at Father's Joel's funeral. Jenny tried to ignore her.

Alisa: Jenny, what happened?

Jenny whispered to Alisa: Manahimik ka, ha! Kung hindi, ikaw ang susunod! (You better zip it! Or you'll be next!).

Alisa not even budging: Ah, ganoon. Marunong akong lumaban, Jenny. At katabi ko lagi and Dios. (Oh, this is how you are now. I know how to fight, Jenny. And God is always on my side.)

Jenny left and slammed her car door shut and drove off.

Then, Alisa could hear loud sirens, not from the church, but from a distance.

Police officers arrived. Then barangay officers turned up to advise everyone that Lake Bito is on red alert – a massive flooding is now out of control due to Lake Bito overflowing. The officers directed the public to the emergency location.

The Elins sent a message to Martin that he is needed at Lake Bito. Martin arrived at the townhall where most people gathered. It seems very organised, and most people are calm.

As Martin looks for Alisa, he overheard some staff from the mayor's office that CIEL has sued DENR and the mayor for corruption and negligence and that CIEL also demand compensation for those affected by the flood. Martin smiles as he keeps looking for Alisa.

Half a day passed. The Elins also started looking for Alisa. They could not find her, anywhere.

Chapter 25 – Driest Darkest Forest

Two short muscular men walk along a dry forest in Mount Pangasugan which is about 1 hour and 20 minutes' drive from Lake Bito.

It's daytime, the forest is so dry that all the two men could hear is the cracking sticks, leaves and branches under their feet as they walk. They are checking out the area. There's not a single sound of birds or insects. All the trees are dry and dead. The dead trees cover about 18 acres of the forest.

A native man noticed the two men and the native told them that the trees have been burned off. That a foreigner bought the land from the council. The buyer wanted to clear the land so he could plant avocado trees. He believed that avocados are in short supply in the western world. However, the buyer was going through a divorce and abandoned his plan.

One of the men started peeling the bark off one of the trees. He kept peeling. Suddenly, he stopped and stepped right back from the tree. Inside the tree, are hundreds of beetles. The beetles have been quietly eating whatever is left of the trees.

Jenny just got home. From the driveway, she could hear her elderly mother speaking with some people. Just as Jenny walked into the living room, two police officers stood up to acknowledge her and they introduced themselves to Jenny.

Police officer: We are here to ask you some questions.
Jenny: I will not say a word without the presence of my lawyer.

The two officers thanked Jenny's mother for serving them coffee as they left.

Jenny contacted the mayor's two bodyguards and then they followed Alisa while she's driving. Jenny and the two men blocked and stopped Alisa on a gravel road. The two men smashed Alisa's window and took and drove her to Mount Pangasugan. At the foot of the mountain, as they got Alisa out of the car, Jenny grabbed a gun from one of the men and shot Alisa on her chest. Alisa fell instantly on the ground. The bodyguards put Alisa in a black plastic sack and sealed it with a rope. They then took Alisa up the hill to the dry forest. It is still daylight, so Jenny is on the lookout in case any of the natives see them. The men started digging deep into the ground. They put a 6-feet metallic water tank in the hole and burned Alisa's body inside it.

While the Elins and Martin look for Alisa. Kristian pulled Gustav aside.

Kristian: I could see smoke. Alisa is on fire!
Gustav: We have been beaten by darkness. Go! See what we can do!

Kristian got to the forest: It's too late.

Jenny and the men just left the forest. They had sealed Alisa's body with cement inside the tank, then covered the whole thing with soil and dry branches.

Kristian looked on the ground as he cries: I'm so sorry Alisa.

Kristian felt a big thump on his right shoulder. A dark spirit just letting him know that they won this battle. Kristian got very angry. Then, he could see from the ground a part of Alisa's body that was not covered with cement – it's her right hand. He took Alisa's burned hand and flew to Norway. He sealed it in a vacuum pack and buried it deep in a frozen lake.

Chapter 26 – To the Other World

While Martin and the Elins were looking for Alisa, Martin knew something was wrong. Martin sat on the floor. He stared at the dirt on the floor. He knew. He knew because he could not feel Alisa's presence in his Soul. His tears were dropping on that dirt on the floor. People surround him just walking around where he is sitting.

Then, Martin looked up through a high window, trying to look at the sky. He got off the floor and went outside. He asked: "And where is Alisa's Soul?"

No answer. No answer from within him, from the Elins or any kind of spirit. Just no answer.

Martin decided to go and see his mother. He found her at the school. She's now working there full-time as an English teacher and guidance councillor.

At night after dinner, Martin's mother was going through old photos of him in her garage. Then she turned on the TV screen and watch some of his Iron Man wins. She smiles as she watched. She is no longer sad.

She went to her kitchen to make a cup of mate tea. Then, she said, "I miss you, Martin. I pray that you are happy where you are." Martin hugged his mum as he cries, "I miss you too, Mum. I wish I could tell you that I found my girl, but she is now gone." He continues, "Mum, will you give me a sign if I should go to the other world?" Martin's mum sips her cup of tea with a quiet smile.

Kristian went back to the frozen lake in Oppstrynsvatnet to ensure that the cells in Alisa's hand are still alive. He flew to a smoky area about 5 kms from the frozen lake. There are at least over one hundred Elins there, gathering for an event.

Martin went out from his mother's house. He run and run as fast and as far as a hundred kms. He is running with anger. He got to a frozen lake and smashed and broke a significant part of the lake.

Martin went back to his mother's home. His spirit is low and tired. His mother fell asleep on the couch holding the remote control and the TV still on. Martin sits opposite his mum, on a lazy boy. As he starts to doze off, he saw a shadow hovering around his mother. Martin stood up and went closer to his mum. The shadow started to put its hands on his mother's forehead. Martin grabbed the shadow's hands and pulled it away.

Martin: What are you? Who are you?
Shadow: You! You failed! You failed all the living things on Earth!
Martin: Who in the world are you? And stay away from my mother! If you have a problem with me, then deal with me! Leave my mother alone!

The shadow started slamming itself against the walls, the floor, and the ceiling.

Shadow: You failed me. You pushed me to be brave, but you failed to protect me. You were supposed to protect me, Martin!
Martin: I don't know who you are!
Shadow: I could feel you. I knew you were there. I felt you each time I stared on the bathroom mirror!

As Martin looked on the shadow. Its head started to show the shape of Alisa's hair. Then, her body. Except, Alisa's shadow is breathing with anger, and she is 8-feet tall.

Alisa's shadow pushed Martin. Martin bumped the foot of the lazy boy and that woke up his mother. She turned the TV off and went to bed.

Alisa's eyes went navy blue, and Martin could see how angry she is. She slapped, punched, and pushed him but he did not block or fight back. Martin let Alisa's anger out.

Then, she fell on the floor, crying. Martin pulled her up and held her. A few minutes passed; Alisa's shadow shrunk to her normal size.

Martin: I'm so sorry, Alisa.
Alisa said nothing.
Martin: Wait, where is your right hand.
Alisa: A dark spirit told me you would know.
Martin: Dark spirit? What! You are co-operating with a dark spirit now?
Alisa: I cannot go to the other world while a part of me is still alive.
Martin: This is crazy! You hand is still alive?

Alisa's eyes started to go blue again.
Alisa: Who are you working for? Tell me where my hand is!
Martin: Alisa, you're behaving like a child.
Alisa: I need to bury my hand so that I can then leave and see Father Joel.
Martin: I do not know where it is, Alisa.

Alisa screamed so loud that it lightly shook the whole house. She retransformed to a darker 8-feet shadow, left, and slammed the door. Martin followed her outside. He saw two shadows follow her.

Martin: What have I done?

Martin lay down beside his mum, hugged her and cried himself to sleep.

Chapter 27 – While Our Hearts are Broken

Martin could hear his mother's thoughts, letting him know to stay and she is advising him not to make decisions during dark or down times.

The Elins had not shown up. It's been six months. Martin spent a lot of time overseeing his mother.

Martin has been keeping his anger inside. Instead of lashing out, he instead goes for walks or run in the forests.

During the beginning of June, he run around Bolzano, northern Italy. It's spring. Martin watched a woman making ravioli with sage and ricotta. She's making it on top of a thick slab of wooden table outside her garden. Martin thought what a sweet life she has. The woman is smiling smelling the scent of roses, sage and rosemary from her garden. Martin noticed a wide tree filled with red fruit. He walked over. It's a pomegranate tree with a huge trunk.

The woman is terribly gorgeous. Her turquoise eyes are in stark contrast with her dark wavy hair and her fair milky skin. She wears a wraparound apron which reveals her small waistline.

Martin then sat slowly on the ground. He felt a thug of overwhelming sadness. The shape of the woman's hair reminded him of Alisa.

Martin then stood up and walked away from the woman. At a café, he noticed a couple of Filipino tourists sitting having lunch. The mother is eating with a big smile on her face. While her son, probably around 14 years old, is trying to eat his salmon and salad dish, while he talks to his dad on the phone.

Martin thought of Lake Bito. He felt anger towards the Elins. They have not shown up despite his calls in the last six months.

So, he runs. He run and he ended up in the Dolomites. Martin hiked and climbed towards Tre Cime di Lavaredo. The well-known three peaks in the Dolomites. He brushed his strong thighs against the soft yellow alpine flowers. Small white butterflies move in motion with Martin. He wonders: Can they see or feel me? Such a contract with the dry surrounding of the Tre Cime next to the layers of lush green landscape and turquoise stream.

Martin feels an immense sense of peace within himself. He climbs and sits on top of the middle Cime. There, he prays. That, he hasn't done in a long while. He prayed that Alisa has moved away from the dark spirits and that she has found her missing hand. That she has gone to the other world to meet Father Joel. Martin sits on the peak for three hours. He has found a way to let Alisa go. Martin closed his eyes and had a flashback of what the Elins told him about what true love is.

Martin went down from the Cime slowly, breathing in and gulping fresh air as he expands his rib cage outwards. The bottom part of Tre Cime is quite sandy. As Martin lifts his right foot, something got entangled around his shoe. He thought it was a bracelet. He brushed out the sand off his shoes and he lifted the stringy object. It's a white rosary. Martin assumed someone, maybe a tourist, must have dropped it here. Martin walked to the nearby Refugio, but it's closed. Martin put the rosary inside the left pocket of his shirt.

Amelia kept in touch with Alisa's parents and Rebecca, Alisa's sister. They assisted each other with their grief over the last six months. Amelia has got Rebecca to volunteer at the cacao plantation in Queensland. Rebecca volunteers at least one weekend a month. Rebecca has become good friends with Bryan. After a few months, Alisa's parents started volunteering as well.

Bryan had organised for his former colleagues from the slaughterhouse in the US to volunteer at the cacao plantation. What Amelia and

Michael started, is now a community whose objective is to make people feel better and make the earth greener.

Amelia, while still working at the farm in Melbourne, flies out regularly to Queensland. All her annual leave and weekends are spent between the Amazon, the Philippines and Queensland.

Amelia and Michael have been invited to present their findings about the Yanomami microbiota. Amelia will present her personal experience about how the microbiota significantly changed her life. The community that invited them is Reserve 1202. A reserve which is managed by a group of scientists from around the world. Reserve 1202 is a 25 acre, almost perfect square of untouched rainforest surrounded by water in the Amazon. Reserve 1202 is the longest running operation of conservation.

After Michael and Amelia's presentation, the scientists asked them to collaborate with Reserve 1202 to somehow mix in the Yanomami's microbiome into the natural compost in the reserve forests. Of course, Michael said yes straight away. Amelia pinched Michael's left leg discretely and she informed the scientists that she and Michael would like a collaborative trade off. That is, to allow them to take some small plants and trees from the reserve. The objective is to grow them in, Queensland, Melbourne, New Zealand and the Philippines.

Two of the six scientists started speaking to each other in Portuguese. They excused themselves, went outside, and proceeded with their discussion there for a few minutes. The two scientists went back in the room and shook Amelia and Michael's hands. They said yes, and confirmed with Amelia that she would have to arrange the transfer of the small plants and trees with the relevant authorities and governments.

Alisa's father, Carlo, with his head now full of grey hair, has been working hard to collaborate with the government officials and businessmen in the Philippines. Along with his wife Cora, decided to carry out Alisa's mission. They are making gains with the support and respect from the younger generation group of elite businessmen. The advantage is that these men can highly influence the decisions made in the senate.

In only four weeks, the plants from Reserve 1202 arrived in the forest where Alisa was killed. After the monsoon rain season, the community found it easy to dig out all the dead trees. There was not a trace of the beetles. Carlo and his team of volunteers planted 6,000 plants and trees in the once dry forest. These included all the plants donated by the businessmen along with three different types of cacao plants.

Carlo and Cora were managing the funding from the businessmen and have organised to employ trusted locals and natives to look after the plants. Alisa's parents interchangeably visit the forest and rostered Amelia, Rebecca and Bryan to also visit the forest. Michael was also allowed to bring in his compost experiment that contain the Yanomami microbiome.

Amelia and Michael were faced with so much barrier when trying to get the Reserve plants into Australia as they have very strict rules on biosecurity.

While sitting in an airplane, Amelia could easily spot, empty spaces of land where native trees have been logged. Particularly, where pine trees have been cut down. Amelia and Michael found out that pine trees are cut down for Rosin and its chemical components to sell to companies that make soaps, varnishes, sealing wax, printer ink, adhesives, binders and gloss oil for paint. The logging companies are not replacing the trees. They cut and go. Amelia and Michael are up against a group of businessmen who propose to turn the empty land to graze cows and sheep.

Months passed. Amelia and Michael's persistence rewarded them with the arrival of the plants from the Amazon Reserve. The government turned around their decision in collaboration with the lawyers of the Bob Brown Foundation.

The 'Soulhaugen' group are well underway making incremental progress. The group have integrated Rudy - Amelia's grandfather, Pablo

-Magdalena's abuelo, Koshi - Yoshi's grandfather. Instead of resting, they are all outdoors, assisting with growing forest on the land.

Chapter 28 – The Cyclic Trap of Money

Jim and a few of his mates are in the boardroom to attend Yoshi's presentation. There were also a couple of representatives from the XiClear Group.

Yoshi is using an unconventional strategy to connect with the investors. The boardroom is surrounded with glass walls. The guests are sitting looking at the heavy rainfall outside. Sean sits next to Yoshi. Yoshi stayed seated with his journal in front of him. A remote control by his right hand.

Yoshi started by saying thank you to the investors for showing their interests. Then he explained that his mission is not to make a lot of money. Yoshi politely informed the attendees that they are welcome to leave if their intention is to purely make money.

One of the potential investors asked: What is your main mission then, Yoshi?

Yoshi: While the business needs to stay viable and sustainable, my mission is to contribute to the reduction of the number of sick people in Australia. It's first line of product being my plant-based cheese creations.

Another potential investor asked: How would that be measured?

We can organise a group that allows them to study customers' blood test results unanimously, before and after consumption of our products. Other customers can choose to simply put their narrative findings about their health.

Yoshi: I realise this kind of strategy is the first. The reality is that Australia and the rest of the western world are getting sicker and sicker. We could no longer rely on our leaders to act. Ordinary people and businesses like us need to take a grass-root revolution on food and the time is now.

Adult-onset diabetes has been renamed to type 2 diabetes because children as young as 5 are diagnosed with it.

70% of the world supply of food are owned by 10 large corporations and they are only driven by profit. It seems that their intention is to keep us addicted to bad food to make further profits. For example, the addictive substance in dairy cheese such as casomorphin, which has the protein called casein. When eaten, casein goes to our blood then to our brain and it attaches the same receptors that heroin or morphine would attach to our brain [3].

The day before, Sean mentioned to Yoshi that one of the potential investors is a large shareholder of insurance companies. Yoshi started drawing a flow chart on his journal. As the men moved closer to see what Yoshi is drawing and writing on his journal, Yoshi explained that consumption of his food creations will eventually lead to the reduction of insurance claims due to sickness, disability and death. Yoshi informed that insurance companies in the US and Canada are already funding projects like ours to significantly reduce the number of claims.

Yoshi further explained that one of the solutions to health is to change our environment so that members of the community have a choice to eat good food and to allow their bodies to move. We need to have an open-sourced decentralised system which allows people to have access to good food within their reach.

Yoshi started to draw a map with a couple of streets on his journal. Street that includes organic farmers' market, community kitchens that facilitate cooking lessons and artisanal food stalls that are permanently installed.

Yoshi then turned on the large screen on the wall. Showing the investors that this type of open-sourced access to fresh and good food is already happening in Italy. He also showed the plant-based cheese makers in

Geneva, Switzerland and Arezzo in Tuscany, Italy. Yoshi then turned off the screen.

As the men turned around, Yoshi explained that his intention is not to make billions and billions of plant-based cheeses all within his company. His intention is to allow other town and communities to learn how to make plant-based cheese on their own to provide for their own community.

Yoshi: The solution is to give each community the knowledge, the skills, the tools, and resources, be it land plus community kitchen. This way, we take back food sovereignty within each community. We will build the business in a way that it makes profit for the purpose of building another business to the next town. I can already see the significant reduction in family's spending on medications, clinics and hospitals. Hospitals would have a lot less patients. Mental health issues would also significantly decrease.

The men are impressed with Yoshi's idea. They said no. They stood up and shook Yoshi's hand. The insurance company investor told him "Good luck."

Jim stayed and shook Yoshi's hand too. He said, "Good luck, Yoshi." Jim nudged Yoshi on his right shoulder and further said "Good luck to us! I'm in! I haven't told you yet that my mother died of complications of diabetes. What you're doing is very admirable."

Chapter 29 – The Invasive Species

The ice at Lake Oppstrynsvatnet, in the Vestland county, Norway, is melting fast. A few days later, Flooding across Victoria, Australia unfold on October 16 in the upper Maribyrnong River.

During that week was the time when Amelia found the human-like hand inside a vacuum-packed bag. The police handed the 'hand' over to the coroner for investigation. It has been kept in the freezer.

The Elins then transformed the 'hand' so that it is coated with dried beetroot roots and skin. The coroner sent it to Symbio Laboratories for further study. The lab results stated that it is a dried crapaudine beetroot. The coroner and the lab informed the police about the test results. The police then rang the head farmer if they would like it back or they will dispose of it.

Amelia told the head farmer she would like it back as she is very curious as to how she perceived it as a human hand. Amelia gave it to Michael to study and test it. Michael is impressed and puzzled about the dried beetroot as it seems to contain one of the most diverse microbiotas, which includes the ones that can only be found in the Northern Hemisphere, the equator and the Southern Hemisphere. The Elins are around while Michael is doing the testing. They recall that Martin's spiritual microbes were transferred to Alisa while Martin held her hand to sleep. Alisa's hand contained the microbes which she received while she lived in the Philippines and New Zealand.

The Elins gave Michael the idea to add Alisa's hand microbes with the ones from the 100-year-old Yanomami woman. Then, mix this compost to the plantations they manage and at the Reserve at the Amazon. The special mix, which is now called the 'Miracle Compost', alternatively called 'Soul Soil' has grown the trees in Australia, the Philippines, the Amazon and New Zealand, fivefold.

On the way back from the Dolomites, Martin swam in Lake Garda, along the village of Cavedine, Trento. While in the water, the Elins follow him. On his right side, four dark shadows hover over him. The white rosary inside Martin's pocket started to light up. Then it would go dark blue and black. Interchangeable changing its colour.

The Elins lifted Martin higher, with water from his Soul dripping down to Lake Garda and the surrounding Monte Bondone. The four dark shadows then face Martin about two metres away. Suddenly, the shadows sucked the white rosary out of Martin's pocket.

Alisa's dark shadow started to appear from the rosary. She stood with her head hanging low juxtaposition to the other shadows. The shadows explained to Alisa that the Elins set her up right from the start. Alisa's eyes started turning dark blue.

The Elins explained to Alisa that humans have become an invasive species. That Mother Nature will always make invasive species extinct. That the world needs both Martin and her to assist in saving humanity.

Martin looked Alisa straight into her eyes. Telling her through her Soul that 'We need you. We still love you. I still love you, Alisa.' Martin and the Elins gave her flashbacks of all the good things that love brought her.

Alisa's eyes transformed from dark blue to bright white. The dark shadows flew away one by one.

Alisa's liver is glowing fiery red. She still has anger trapped inside her. Martin cried to let his own anger out too. Martin held Alisa tight until the fire in her liver subsided and disappeared.

The Elins surround Martin and Alisa and flew them higher up into the atmosphere.

Alisa and Martin let go of their cherished outcomes, one by one. Every single one of them. Then, they realised they are floating and could fly on their own.

While Martin is still holding Alisa, all her dried burned skin started to peel away. Her burned skin started to strickle down the lake, to our earth while it spins around its axis, to the land, the mountains, the rivers, the oceans.

Martin held Alisa until she is mostly made of light, her Soul.

The Elins directed Michael, Amelia and the rest of the Soulhaugen team where Alisa's 'Soul Soil' are located. Jacob is now a qualified ranger; he can go to exchange programs overseas, carefully spreading the Soul Soil. Magdalena continues to be a champion for Mission Blue, now mostly swimming and diving to deposit the Soul Soil in oceans, rivers and streams.

The team Soulhaugen continue their work, toward humanity's protopian world.

Chapter 30 – The Incremental Move

While at the cacao plantation in Queensland, Australia, Michael and Amelia are having lunch with Rudy, Pablo and Kiyoshi. Michael asked the question; Why do most people cannot see the urgency that we need to co-operate with Mother Nature?

Kiyoshi answered: It's not that because most people are stupid, it's because most people are too close to see what is happening to their surroundings. Most are too drowned into their own routines.

Rudy nodding: And of course, most people are unaware they are highly brainwashed by marketing and consumerism.

While Pablo is staring into space with some joy in his eyes and a big smile on his face, Amelia brushes her own hands on her upper arms and shoulders and said: Yes, most people are too close to see, and some can see, but they chose to close, you know, they go into a denial state, because it is easier to turn a blind eye. Amelia feels the presence of Alisa's Soul and she's not aware that Martin is there too. Amelia excused herself and went to the kitchen. Just as she slides the thick slab of wooden door, it screeked slightly.

Alisa whispered to her: Tell Rudy that you are taking him to the Acacia Healthcare's Extraordinary General Meeting (EGM). Amelia is bemused as she's never heard of Acacia Healthcare. She presumes that Rudy has some shares with this company.

Mid-morning of 28 January 2025, Acacia's directors and key management personnel line up at the registration desk. On the right side of the desk, two staff members of the company, offer some free merchandise with the company's logo on them ¬ large umbrellas, mouse pads, car windscreen sun blockers. While the executives prepare for their presentation, shareholders who arrived early and have registered are enjoying their cup of tea and coffee at the lobby.

One of the resolutions during the EGM is about the potential takeover of another major pharmaceutical distributor The Collab Chemist, pending approval of ACCC (Australian Competition and Consumer Commission).

At the venue's driveway, Acacia's Chief Financial Officer (CFO), Kyran Singh, looks back to ensure that his Rolls Royce is being parked carefully by the staff member. Kyran then goes to a revolving door. The door starts to jolt and feels like it is stuck. He turned behind him and saw a boy who is about 8-9 years old. Kyran is rather confused as this boy seem to resemble him when he was young.

Boy: What are you doing? You got us stuck!
Kyran: I beg your pardon, little man?
Boy: You've got to move. Go!
Kyran is very annoyed and frowned at the boy.
Boy: No! Don't just look at me! You've got to change and make a move!
Kyran now feeling anxious: Ah, what?
Boy pointing at Kyran's other foot: Change your next step and move!
The boy carried on: If you don't make a move, I will be late for my presentation! You are impacting my future right now!

Kyran is unaware that Alisa guided the boy there.

The door finally turned around again. Kyran proceeded to the registration desk and took his name badge. Kyran is then called to present the Acacia's key financial results. Though he was bothered with the boy's attitude earlier, he stood tall and confident behind the lectern and his presentation went well.

Just as Kyran is about to sit with the rest of the executives in the panel, Rudy stood up and shouted out a question: Sir, where are all the profits really going and what is it truly for? Amelia tried to get him to sit and said: Opa, it's not question time yet. The Company Secretary tried to get the cameras to stop rolling.

Rudy: No, keep the camera and the audio rolling please. This is a very important question.

Kyran put his hand up to signal: It is okay. I will answer the question.

'Sir, the profits are there so we could expand the company and so that you, and all the other shareholders would benefit from higher dividends and yield in your investment in Acacia.

Rudy calmly said thank you and proceeded: That part I understand. However, most of the medications the company is selling are just there to suppress the symptoms. Can you not see how our society is at the moment? So many people are sick, even the youngest of our children. Sir, I must tell you that buying that other company will only make Acacia have absolute power in its industry. I do not want any more money at the expense of our children's health. I must tell you that, it is not the right move. I ask you, Sir, to please do the right thing.

Amelia is unaware that Martin is guiding Rudy to be brave.

The following week, Kyran resigned from Acacia. Thirteen weeks later, he made phone calls and arranged personal meetings. He gathered key community leaders including doctors, nurses, builders, parents, nutritionists, molecular biologists, organic farmers, teenagers and children as young as 9.

Eight months later, Kyran, his key leaders and dedicated staff have built what is called 'Life Recipe'. Life Recipe is a community-based group with its mission to proactively reduce the number of sick people in their community. A community that helps each other to heal.

Five years later, a journalist is in town called Upper Ferntree Gully, trying to interview people in the streets. The journalist came across one of the doctors at Life Recipe.
Journalist: We've looked at the statistics of the number of people with diabetes in this town. It seems that in the last five years, there has been at least 70% reduction of the number of people with diabetes. We hear narratives that people here have reversed their diabetes. What do you think may have happened?

Doctor Vedeshwar: As a doctor, before the incremental change in this town, I felt very hypocritical. I was a doctor who used to prescribe medications to my client with the same medications that I was on.

Journalist: Oh, and I presume that you are about to say that you no longer take any medications.

Doctor Vedeshwar: That is correct. I've been off the medication for 2 and a half years now.

Journalist: How do you think that happened?

Doctor Vedeshwar: Well, look around you. Our community has incrementally transformed most of our streets with many options of good food, many places to walk, bike and exercise. We have many free community kitchens where people exchange cooking ideas. We've strategically made it easier for our people to eat better and move our bodies. We care for and educate each other, either one-on-one or as a group. Over the last five years, we helped and funded most of the junk and addictive food businesses transition to a good food business or distributor. There are some who left town, and then there are some who became organic farmers.

Chapter 31 – Cielo

Alisa is peacefully flying toward the cirrus clouds with the sunrise peeking behind it. Her white dress flowing coalesce within the cool clouds. As she goes higher, she whispers *Cielo, my love is only for Cielo.* The Sky.

Martin watches her quietly. Alisa slowly and deeply breaths in some of the clouds. He then held her, his strong hands around her waistline. Her long wavy hair flowing over Martin's shoulder. They both smile. They watch our Earth from above. Their eyes fill with sadness.

They perceive humans as if they are all 2-year-olds over consuming ice-cream until they vomit, making a big mess. The sand is being taken from rivers, resulting to collapsing ecology and communities nearby. They see 65 million newly built flats sitting empty in China.

Martin and Alisa flew over to 'The Palm' in Dubai. They are shaking their head as the manmade islands of about 300 sit mostly empty. They flew over to Singapore viewing how its land is being extended using illegal sand mining from Cambodia, Indonesia and Vietnam. They flew back up to Cielo. Carefully investigating the groups of people who are doing their best to sustain our Earth.

Alisa is flying toward Caridad National High School. A nearby school in Lake Bito. She gave visions about sand mining in Lake Bito to 8 schoolteachers. They started to do a lot of reading. During the weekend, the teachers gathered and headed for Lake Bito at 4.00am. There, they witnessed the suction of the sand.

The teachers changed their lesson plans. They instructed the students to read 'Sand' by Michael Welland and 'The World in a Grain' by Vince Beiser. Over the next two weeks, the classes carefully discussed the facts from the books. During the last 15 minutes of each lesson, they watch a documentary by ENDEVR called 'The Sand Mafia'. At the end of two weeks, the students are allocated into groups of 8. Their task is to debate and summarise the pros and cons of sand mining, and what solutions they will act upon.

The students discussed what they've learnt during dinner with their parents. A very articulate and stubborn 16-year-old boy, Nathaniel Manalo, asked questions to his affluent parents: "Why do we need such a big house using so much cement? It's just the three of us here in this big mansion."

Alisa recognised Nathaniel's ability to feel what he views as injustice; he feels guilt within him. Nat is losing sleep. Alisa guides him to be brave so that he acts upon the uncomfortable feeling of dissonance.

"Nat didn't go to school today." His mother is trying to explain to his father. "His teacher just rang me to say that they could not find him at school, and I told them that he is not at home. I'm going to the barangay leader and ask them to help us find him."

Nat has been at Lake Bito since 4.30am. He is trying to stop the suction of the sand.

Over the next few weeks. Nat organised with his friends and school acquaintances to barricade and video the sand mining at Lake Bito. Oh yeah, they had the works! DJI 3 mini-pro and other gadgets their parents never imagine would exist. The teenage girls and boys who are operating the three drones are hidden within tall trees in separate locations. They each have another 'buddy' at the foot of each tree with a laptop. Each drone team pass or drop and catch carefully the two tiny alternate microSDXC. So that the buddy then can crop the video and upload it to their social media accounts. Tagging all relevant accounts. The videos went viral. Almost 13 million people watch the videos as the event upfold. After five hours, Nat and his team managed to stop the sand mining.

Their parents are fuming. It's 9.30am at school. The eight teachers just left their schools without letting reception know. They joined Nat and his team. They rang their family and friends to organise tents, food and water. They asked the whole community to join this memorable grass root movement. Their message stated, "It is our duty to fight for our Nature and our future."

Nat is standing in the middle of the land near the water of Lake Bito. The land resembles the core of the moon. The drone drops right in front of him as he says: "No one is doing anything about this rolling problem of sand mining. How many more floodings do we have to endure? How many more of us must live with bronchitis from the sand debris floating in our air? Each one of us is responsible to stop this sand war and put life back to Lake Bito. Who's joining me right now?" Nat continues, "Hindi na kami bulag! Hindi na kami duwag! (We're no longer blind; We're no longer cowards!). My ancestors fought for my freedom! We want freedom from the abuse of our surrounding! We are here fighting for our lives and our future!"

Despite strong opposition, many meetings and debates between the school, parents and the council; Nat and his team persisted. After a couple of weeks, the mayor of Lake Bito and Jenny, are on Channel 7 News. The footage shows their arrest as the police lead them to the Leyte Regional Prison in Abuyog.

Alisa's parents, Carlo and Cora, has been working behind the scenes with Sean and his partners guided by CIEL (Centre for International and Environmental Law).

Big worldwide news! The CEOs of the companies and politicians, both locally and nationally, involved in the illegal sand mining have also been arrested to join the others at the Abuyog prison.

Over the following months, those who persisted with taking sand are instantly put behind bars.

Nat and his team have collaborated with a team of local lawyers and Sean and his partners, so that the mayor, Jenny and all others who are involved are not given bail.

A community in Lerderderg in Victoria, Australia, organised the same grass roots movements to stop sand mining to save their gorge.

Alisa and Martin are satisfied that a solution to one aspect of the problem is underway to being resolved. They stare at each other's gaze. Quietly agreeing to the deeper root of the problem.

Alisa: The genesis of this problem is the excessive and wasteful demand for sand[5]. No one wants sand mining in their backyard, but they keep supporting the building of large shopping complex and such. The greedy operators will just get the sand somewhere else whenever they can.

Martin: The significant part of the solution is to reduce that demand. We must be patient, Alisa. It's a long path solution and we must keep doing our best. We will be faced with enormous resistance. We must have faith that humanity will gradually evolve from this.

Martin continues: We must whisper to the bystanders, that the activists are asking them to open their minds and hearts, so that they start to see, feel and account for the consequences of doing nothing. The activists are asking them to be open, so that they may feel what the activists feel.

Alisa: Therefore, the solution is to educate humanity to consume less, a lot less! Not just for sand, cement, concrete. Minimise consumption of practically everything!

Alisa and Martin flew over the cities.

Martin: Let's start educating the greedy part of humans. Let us whisper to them every 3.00am, including their children and their grandchildren. Let us organise with the Elins to 'drop bricks on their heads'. Perhaps give them serious medical condition, a crisis of some kind. The solution is to have many collaborative actions between the good, the greedy and the ones who are stuck in their daily routine.

Martin started 'working' on major real estate companies in Australia, China, the Philippines, and New Zealand. One of his works is allowing them to dream about the collapse of a major building project in Morocco, mainly made of cement and concrete. Also, showing them in their dreams to get in contact with organisations that are using alternative eco-building materials such as Nightingale Housing in Melbourne, Australia and existing companies that use hemp to produce durable building materials. Martin is also focused on one real estate CEO who has recently been diagnosed with lymph node cancer.

The whole world watch as Lake Bito evolve into a brave and loving community.

Carlo and Cora are in Manila collaborating with the authorities and politicians. They do not meet them in their offices. They meet them at their home. Discussing the possible solutions, during dinner time in the presence of the authorities and politicians' children.

Alisa is joined by the Elins working on the decision makers of building government houses and venues. Alisa and the Elins whispers to them: They do not have to be that big and made of concrete!

Alisa has been whispering to Sean to get councils around the world to collaborate with eco-businesses, researchers and companies that operate with a sustainable and circular business model.

The Souhaugen are working, caring and collaborating globally:

Amelia in Australia. Carlo and Cora in the Philippines, Singapore and other ASEAN countries. Magdalena and Jacob are doing their work and collaborating globally. Michael in South America. Martin's mother in Europe. Sean in New Zealand and globally with his worldwide network. Yoshi in Australia and Japan. Bryan and Rebecca in the USA and recently started with a few connections in Kenya.
Each are peaceful with their own Soul, therefore unafraid of dying. Keeping in mind that their mission is long path, servicing those who have come before them going back hundreds of years. Working hard to educate and give life-changing experiences within their contemporary world, so that the current generation and the next, will carry on with

their mission. They acknowledge that each good step they do now, will lead to other good steps taken by many others.

At Mr Hong's, Martin whispers to Yoshi as Yoshi struggles to put a large bag of used coffee grounds in the rubbish bin.

Martin whispers: Wait! Put it in the fridge for now.

Yoshi is wondering: *I don't have enough space in the fridge. Umm, actually, let's see if I can move things around.*

The next morning, as Yoshi opens Mr Hong, a young gentleman sits outside and waits on the green bench. He smiles at Yoshi and says 'I'm looking forward to having my coffee. I heard it's really good here.' Yoshi rattles the keys, 'Our secret is that we use organic coffee, mate.' The man replied 'Oh even better, for my body and our planet. No rush, mate, just whenever you're ready.'

While Mr Hong's staff gets ready. The man sits as close as possible to Yoshi.

Man: Wow! That cup of coffee is truly one to remember!
Yoshi: Thanks, man!
Man: What do you do with the coffee grounds after?
Yoshi: Well, to be honest, they've been going in the bin. Though I did save some in the fridge last night. Why?
Man: By the way, my name is Rajii Chand. I'm a researcher for RMIT. My team is currently developing concrete made from coffee grounds and steel by-products, and sometimes we use wood-chip bio-char. The main ingredient is coffee grounds.

Yoshi: I'm happy to give you the bag of coffee grounds I saved last night. Should we make a deal? For every referral you have for someone you know buying one of our plant-based cheeses, I will give you 1 kgs of coffee grounds. How's that?

Rajii, as he shakes Yoshi's hand: Easy deal, mate!

After six months, Yoshi and his big network of restaurants owners are collaborating with Rajii and his team. Both sides are feeling good with the win-win-win collaboration. More revenue for the restaurants, more coffee grounds for RMIT to build and test their 'coffee cement'. This deal has significantly reduced coffee grounds going to landfill as other Australian states follow suit.

Sean and his Melbourne partners organised with the Shire Council, in collaboration with Bild Group, to build a long footpath, along Howey Street, Gisborne, in the Macedon Ranges in Victoria, Australia.

Testing is organised by Sean six months later. The result is that the coffee concrete seems to be 30% stronger than traditional concrete.

Amelia, with the guidance of Alisa, has been acting as project co-ordinator for transitioning concrete companies to use more of coffee concrete. Amelia, during her speech with the concrete building companies emphasized that: "This will take time, and I understand that this is a big ask. We will incrementally transition into using coffee concrete and other eco-building materials. What I am sure of is that we are heading in the right and more loving direction!"

Despite Amelia's busy schedule. She is still working 1 day a week at organic farms. Intentionally picking the days when volunteers attend, so that she can relay her important message, hoping that they will act and create a positive domino effect to those around them. Volunteers come from varied backgrounds – chefs, nurses, technology specialist, grandmothers. Volunteers usually ask Amelia what a normal Joe Blogg can do to help our Earth. The common comment is that they are overwhelmed with all the information available, they get confused and so they end up doing nothing. Amelia advised them to start at home, for example, replacing their paper towel with a clean tea towel, to always take a refillable cup when buying coffee, to use renewable electricity instead of gas, to grow what we eat. Then, join a couple of groups that are strong advocates for animal protection, ocean and soil. Amelia further emphasises: You will be surprised how much each of us can help by starting with such small steps. The trick is to stick to the Japanese word 'Kaizen'. We must continuously improve from each step. One small step will eventually lead to significant impact. But the most important thing I can tell you is that each of us must reduce consumption. That can be from building large houses unnecessarily down to the brand of toilet paper we buy. We can all look at our garage first to see if we can use or fix something from there before deciding to buy something new.

Alisa and Martin watch our world from Cielo. Many small pockets of the world have progressed.

Alisa: For those who are paralysed with their daily routines, let us ask the Elins to wake them up! Perhaps, an accident, a sickness, a divorce, a death of a loved one. Our job is to guide them to finally overcome their excuses and indolence.

Martin: Will they start to listen to our whispers?

Chapter 32 – The Loss that Swelled into a Win

Alisa and Martin flew over to Leyte Regional Prison in Abuyog. They watched Jenny doing some weeding in the prison veg garden. She's talking to a prison mate who is beside one end of a 50-meter garden bed full of rows of okra and talong (eggplant).

Jenny sat on the edge of the garden bed behind her, sighing, while trying to fit both her legs in the lower gap between two no dig garden beds.

Jenny is very upset: I really regret being a part of sand mining. How did I not know it is a form of stealing. You know, thou shall not steal! I've been going to the chapel to beg for forgiveness.

Prison mate: We made mistakes, Jenny. Sometimes, our poverty leads us in the wrong and dark direction.

Jenny as she cries: And I killed Alisa! I'm so freaking scared that I will go to hell when I die!

The prison mate tried to change the subject because she doesn't want to get upset herself: Where do the stolen sand go to anyway?

Jenny: All I know is that it goes to Western Australia, somewhere along Timor Sea. But the other bodyguard said it's going to Montana. So maybe, the sand goes to both Australia and USA to build houses made of concrete.

Alisa and Martin flew approximately 230 kms toward the Northwest coast of Australia, near the Timor Sea. There sit - Mandara Oil Field.

It's cloudy and the night is in deep darkness.

Alisa: What does sand have to do with this area? Are they building made-made islands here too?

Martin: No, come, look!

Martin sees sparking lights ahead. Alisa squints her dark brown eyes to make sense of the 200-tonne platform just ahead of them. As they flew closer, they hear large machineries and working men grunting as they lift and shift machineries. The men are wearing khaki overalls, white hard hats, one hat filled with colourful stickers. They wear work boots, protective glasses. The men have traces of dust and splatters of some oil on their faces.

Martin recognised two men among the workers. They're friends of Bryan originally from Albert Lea, Minnesota. They enjoyed working at the Cacao plantation in Queensland. They have family to support back in the US, so they opted to work here in the oil and gas field, assisting in fracking.

Fracking is a process where rocks are fracked to access oil and gas. Sand is one of the main ingredients of fracking. The type of sand that is 95% coarse. Fracking is a mixture of sand, water and toxic chemicals. The sand is needed to keep the rocks open.

Alisa: That's it? I got murdered for this?

Martin immediately thought that Alisa's eyes might become dark blue again.

Alisa reading Martin's Soul, while stroking the side of his hair: Don't worry. I've evolved from that!

Then, an alarm goes off - beep, beep, beep. The workers keep working. They know it's only the alert tone. After 20 seconds of beeps, the alarm was followed by a high pitch sound which goes whoop, whoop, whoop. It's the evacuation tone.

Alisa suddenly disappeared.

Martin then sees a 3-second flash fire which started to burn a worker's hands and arms. A supervisor quickly used the fire extinguisher to help the worker. Martin pulled, guided and gathered Bryan's friends and the other workers over to the evacuation area.

A ruptured gas pipeline ignited. In a nano second, followed by an explosion. The explosion disconnected the power and ventilation. It sends rocks and debris that weighs up to 17 kgs flying up into the air.

A few men are injured. Everyone made it to the lifeboats. Martin is flying behind the men as they watch Mandara Oil & Gas Field from a distance. Two hours later, as the men bowed their heads down to step over the rescue boats, two more Mandara pipelines exploded.

Martin knows where Alisa is. As soon as the alarm went off, she dived into the sea. Using her dance moves that she knows would make her swim faster, she alerted the sea creatures to swim alongside her. Many of them made it to Exmouth Gulf, where one of Mission Blue's hope spot is located.

It took 75 days to clean up the oil spill and the debris from the sea. Despite efforts from Mission Blue's staff, including Magdalena and Jacob, about an eighth of the sea creatures died from the incident. Among those who lost their lives[6] are:

- Pygmy blue whales (endangered)
- Blue whale (endangered)
- Sei whale (endangered)
- Fin whale (endangered)
- Grey nurse shark (vulnerable)
- Great white shark (vulnerable)
- Whale shark (vulnerable)
- Dugong (other protected fauna)
- Green turtle (vulnerable)
- Loggerhead turtle (endangered)
- Hawksbill turtle (vulnerable)6
- Olive ridley turtle (endangered)
- Flatback turtle (vulnerable)

- Leatherback turtle (vulnerable)
- Dusky sea snake (endangered)
- Shortfin mako (endangered)
- Longfin mako (endangered)
- Green sawfish (vulnerable)
- Largetooth sawfish (vulnerable)
- Short-nosed sea snake (critically endangered)
- Olive python (vulnerable)
- Northern quoll (endangered)
- Ghost bat (vulnerable)
- Greater bilby (vulnerable)
- Pilbara leaf-nosed bat (vulnerable)
- Australian lesser noddy (endangered)
- Abbott's booby (endangered)
- Eastern curlew (critically endangered)
- Curlew sandpiper (critically endangered)
- Red knot (endangered)
- Great knot (critically endangered)
- Greater sand plover (vulnerable)
- Lesser sand plover (endangered)
- Bar-tailed godwit (vulnerable)
- North Siberian bar-tailed godwit (critically endangered)
- Southern giant petrel (endangered)
- Australian painted snipe (endangered)
- Australian fairy tern (vulnerable)
- Night parrot (critically endangered)

The residents of Exmouth, Onslow, Northwest Cape, and Learmonth, in collaboration with Greenpeace AP, submitted a case against Mandara. The case is discontinued due to legal technicalities.

Martin whispered to Sean and Kevin to arrange an urgent meeting with their colleagues to find out who would join them in representing the case against the directors of Mandara. Kevin is leading the meeting. The group of 10, mostly in their 20s and 30s surround Kevin as he spoke calmly.

Kevin: Here are the main points of the case[6]:

1. The directors knew their assets are aging.
2. There are records of near-miss of worker fatalities which reflect improper engineering practices.
3. Safety is compromised due to Mandara CEOs focus on cost-cutting.
4. We will find a strategy to show the world that this industry is in a race to earn profits for their shareholders as the world transition from fossil fuel to renewable energy.
5. Finally, what is our case's mantra?

The youngest of the lawyers said: Enough of the Greed!

Unlike a TV series where a case is finished in a few weeks, the group, which they now call themselves as '10' worked on the case with their heart and Soul. Three years on; '10' lost. The oil and gas industry's lobbying and payoff to the politicians are too strong.

Martin and Alisa whispered to Magdelena and Jacob. They woke up in the middle of the night and drove to Northwest Cape along the east of Timor Sea. They took some samples of the sea water. Jacob drove it to Michael while he is in Australia.

Michael found a cocktail of toxic chemicals in the water sample, including carcinogenic radium 226 and uranium. Test results also showed traces of butoxyethanol, ethylhexamol and glutaraldehyde.

The Soulhaugen gathered in Yoshi's restaurant, most in person, some online. Magdalena mentioned that she noticed a few people walking around the beach wearing bandana on their heads. She presumed they are going through some medical treatment. After the meeting, Sean approached team '10' and they gathered along Northwest Cape.

Martin and Alisa are guiding some members of the public at the beach and whispering to them that it is okay to speak with the members of '10'. The public are well aware of the growing number of cancer patients in the last 3 years. In fact, many of the children are asking their parents and teachers why this is happening.

'10' gathered notes, names and contact details of those who are willing to participate in the case against Mandara.

Sean: 10! We've been given a second chance. This is the one that will make the bad players pay back for their greed. This new case is the first time the oil and gas industry are faced with a challenge with evidence outside of their control.

Kevin's phone rang. It's a home phone number from Western Australia (WA). The caller introduced himself as an advisor for the Exmouth Council and stated that he got Kevin's phone number from the grapevine.

Council Advisor (CA): I see you are putting a case against the directors of Mandara.

Kevin: How can I help?

CA: My daughter has bone cancer. She's 16. Despite me repeatedly telling her not to swim in the sea, she's been swimming there in secret from us. Her specialist confirmed there is radium and uranium in her bones and blood. You know where I'm heading?

Kevin: I'm sorry to hear about your daughter.

CA: I'm so sorry. I shouldn't have taken the payoff from them. All that money is not worth my daughter's suffering.

After attending his weekly 12-step program with Alcoholics Anonymous, Kevin called '10' to have an urgent meeting.

Kevin: For this case, what's our mantra? Never mind, I know. For Our Children. That is our mission now – For Our Children.

In collaboration with Greenpeace AP, it took '10' two years to gather evidence. The group has 156 individuals who has agreed to be involved as witnesses. They range from people with cancer, to those with disabilities resulting from gastrointestinal and nervous disorders and those who suffer from chronic bronchitis.

The council advisor's daughter is now 18. In hospital, she spoke very softly. Her evidence is put through a live video permitted by the high court. She explained her own narrative about her experience from swimming in the sea to getting sick often. The colour of her eyes and skin reflects her terminal condition. Beside her bed is her father, on the other, is her doctor. The doctor explained in scientific detail how radium and uranium is eating up her bones. The machine connected to her nose tubes to assist her breath better, is quietly beeping in the background. The doctor excused himself to check on her.

The judge in the court room asked to stop recording and turn off the camera for now. The daughter insisted 'No, keep it rolling please! I want you all to know that the money is not worth all the pain. The pain that my family and friends are carrying for me.

The beeps get louder and faster. The judge said to turn the camera off. The father and daughter said to keep it ON. In a matter of 10 minutes, the jury watched her die in her father's arms. The father, rocking her daughter in his arms, quietly cried, as did each member of the jury.

The father stared straight into the camera, looking shocked and lost, he whispered: Enough of the greed, for my dear child.

For the first time in the history of humanity, the world watched, some in disbelief, most with relief and great hope, as the directors of an oil and gas company are arrested and dropped off at the gates of Casuarina Prison.

The bigger news is that Mandara's largest shareholder and fund managers were also arrested because it showed in their auditors and investigators' reports that they knew all along that the chemicals being used during fracking are carcinogenic.

Then, a financial global panic eventuated because share prices plummeted for the fossil industry and all their associated listed companies. Investors turned their funds to renewable listed companies, organic farmers and sustainable start-up businesses.

Chapter 33 – The Secret Resistance Underground

A year has passed. Martin visited his mother in Norway. He then met up with Alisa in Northern Italy. They are taking a rest. They visited the area where Alisa's Soul transcended away from the dark shadows, near the biggest lake in Italy, Lake Garda. They walked. They chased each other, as if they are two young children playing hide and seek.

They head north of Lago di Garda. Now speeding past while trying to avoid the tourists, through Spiaggia di Torbole, entering river Sarca, passing by a group of organic cooperatives exchanging their produce. Martin and Alisa lay down in Riserva Naturale Provincile Marocche in Sarca Valley, breathing in the scent and microbiome from conifer and holly oak forest. They exchanged each other's breath.

They hear the moos of the Pustertaler cows and the bells hanging around their necks. Alisa flew closer to the cows, which are mostly white with splatters of black. Alisa did some dance twirls to add some of her splatters to the cow's skin and to the grass they are eating.

Alisa and Martin flew 56 kms from Lago di Garda and now stand on a small and quiet town of Cavedine. Both are feeling renewed. Alisa feels the heaviness of her responsibilities.

Alisa: There's still so much work to do.

Martin led her to a small winding street via Novembre IV. He takes her left hand and leads her toward the foot of a hill. She looks up to view 12 lights each separated in the same distance, the lights vertically toward a diminutive wooden church – La Madonna della Grotta. A chiesa (church) currently lit up in pink.

Martin: It's pink meaning a girl was born in Cavedine today.

Alisa kept quiet. Martin knows that she's missing her mother, father and sister after seeing the grotto and its flower garden. Alisa puts a pinccone beside the feet of the Madonna. The two slept afloat just above the flower garden.

It's sunrise at 6.30am. The volunteers tending the garden arrive. Alisa and Martin rest and talked for 5 hours. From about 300 metres, Martin spots a young woman from a window staring toward the chiesa. The woman is standing still. She only moved as a black dog jumped on her trying to get her attention.

Martin: I feel that there's something about this woman that is unfolding.

Martin closed his eyes to contact the Elins. The Elins confirmed yes, that woman is an essential instrument.

Alisa and Martin walked up the wooden stairs to the kitchen where the woman is. Her name is Monique. Mon is a WWOOFer. A volunteer for World-Wide Opportunities for Organic Farmers. Mon is in Cavedine for four weeks to assist farmers who grow aromatic herbs, seasonal vegs, and their larger scale produce – forest and organically grown shiitake mushrooms.

Mon plays with the dog with a soccer ball in the kitchen. She then washed her hands and started cooking tagliatelle with spigariello and aglio bianco polesana (a large mild white garlic grown in nearby Veneto). Mon could hear the young farmer couple coming up the stairs. It's Monday, so it's their day off.

Mon: How was your swim?
Female farmer: Molto bene. I feel so refreshed now.
Male farmer: Ah, you feel at home in our villa now. That's smells really good. What are you cooking?
Mon: A simple pasta dish. It will be al dente in about 2 minutes.

Mon and the farmers have dinner while they talked about what happened in the mushroom forest the other day. Mon looked underneath the dining table as the dog tries to get her attention for some food.

Martin listens as the stories unfold and laughter echoes around the kitchen walls. Alisa could feel Mon's heart spilling with joy. Alisa occasionally turns to the kitchen window looking back at the small church from a distance.

Mon and the farmers revised each moment at the mushroom forest the other day. They were busy picking up the wooden logs from the tanks of water. Each log is about 3 feet long and weighs about 8 to 10 kgs. The logs are then stacked with enough gaps between them on the forest ground with the first layer vertically, the next layer horizontally, alternating the layers until a stack is complete and steady totalling up to 11 to 13 logs. The stack of logs is then covered with white cloths. The aim for each day is to make six stacks.

The logs have been drilled with some holes. Mycelia are then spread inside the holes and that's where the mushrooms grow.

The other task for each day is to gather the logs which mushrooms have been harvested from. Each log is then carried individually to be soaked and submerged in the tank of water overnight. Mon and the farmers need to fill six tanks of water each day.

After the fourth tank is filled, Mon heard a barking dog which to her sound unusually loud.

Male farmer: It could be a wolf.

The bark then turned into a growl. Mon and the farmers stayed quiet for a few moments. The growl got louder and more often. Then, they heard fast running steps and dried leaves being moved. The growl echoed upwards around the forest Norway Spruce tall Christmas trees.

Mon walked fast toward the truck, sat down and shut the door. The farmers followed her, and the male farmer rang the forest manager. They recalled the recent news about two local men who encountered wild bears and died.

On the phone, the forest manager informed them that bears, and wolf are normally quiet before they attack. So, he told the farmers to make loud noises, toot the horn of the truck and carry on working.

As Mon and the farmers recall the experience while having their dinner, they laughed as Mon says: That was the fastest two tanks of water we ever filled.

The forest manager rang the farmers the following evening to confirm that the noise was from a red deer. Perhaps being challenged by a wolf. The male farmer looked up and played a video of a red deer from YouTube.

Mon: That's exactly it! Why are we not taught the sound of a deer when we were at school!

Martin took some Arion Rufus, red slugs which swallowed Lisa's Soul Soil a year ago. The big slugs have developed storing diverse microbiome within them. The next day, Martin put the slugs in the basket sitting on the back of the truck. Martin quickly pushed the basket as the male farmer put his red slim pick with a sharp knife at the end. It just missed the slugs. The farmer put the basket beside the water tank in the mushroom forest.

The slugs which the farmer think of as annoying, because they eat parts of the mushrooms, are now spreading their beneficial microbiome in the tank water and the forest. When the logs are soaked, the biomes are further incorporated into the growing of the mushrooms. Soul Soil, which are now eaten by the farmers and Mon. The mushrooms are also eaten by many restaurant customers where the farmers deliver their mushrooms, mainly in and around the Piazza Duomo of Trento.

After a month, Mon's next WWOOFing is in Tasmania, Australia. She is booked to volunteer at a 100% off-grid organic farm, where a compost toilet is used. When the toilet 'load' is full, the head farmer then scoops the load into a large wheelbarrow to be then taken and buried under a deep hole.

Mon's microbiomes are living through the deep hole. It only took a few days for fungus arbuscule mycorrhizae to colonise the nearby plant roots. The fungus trade with trees in exchange for sugar and fats. They get their carbon directly from the trees. The fungus transports nutrients between trees. If one tree is deficient in nitrogen, the fungus gets it from the tree that has excess of it and carry it to the tree that needs it[7].

Alisa: How do these fungi know where and when to trade? How do they calculate how much nutrients to carry?

Martin: I guess they have their own Elins too.
Alisa smiles: Ah, like they also have their own 'Mother of God'.

Martin and Alisa watched the fungus penetrate through the roots of each tree and plant. They spread underground in the forest. The spread slowed down. Then, it stopped. Martin sees a big patch of the forest being cleared in Takayna Forests, where a large-scale logging is happening. Shaving a big part of the forest.

When the logging machineries finally stopped, Alisa hears people speaking loudly with hand-held speakers. Alisa could see from a distance three treehouses just above the canopy of the forest. Each tree house has at least three people in it. Joined by local Tasmania residents are:

Tree 1: Michael and Amelia
Tree 2: Rebecca and Bryan
Tree 3: Carlo and Cora

Each speaker clearly and interchangeably repeating:

We have journalists recording.
Can we speak with the person in charge?
There are swift parrots, koalas, and many other creatures that live in this forest where you are logging. What you are doing is illegal! [8]

They are not getting any response.

Chapter 34 – Receiver of Consciousness

While in Australian, Michael had a call from one of his relatives in the Amazon.

Caller: Marima is very ill. She has been very weak in the last few days and unable to get out of her hammock. She doesn't even want to drink water.

Michael flew over the next day to see his mother.

Michael's most difficult life experience unfolded in a matter of two days. His mother, oldest half-brother and one of his nephews past away.

Later, the biopsy showed high level of mercury in their blood, kidneys and lungs. A few months later, scientists and geologists from the National Geographic are taking buccal and skin swabs, nail clippings and single blood draw from birds, fish, primates, amphibians and reptiles from the jungle. National Geographic reports stated there is mercury contamination among 79% of the subjects they tested. In addition to the animals in the jungle, mercury has also been found in the water and the air. When mercury is burned, it turns into aerosol.

Marima died of central nervous system, kidney and lung disfunction because of high levels of mercury inside her body.

Michael's grief turned into suppressed anger. He is overwhelmed by his resentment towards the illegal gold miners who use mercury to separate gold from rocks and sediments.

Amelia flew to the Amazon to take Michael back to Australia.

Michael fell into deep depression. Not long after that, he received a call from his father, Chris.

Chris: I'm sorry about your mother, Mike. But what you are trying to do there is an impossible mission. Your brain created and imagined that mission when you were young. It's time to come home. You will be safe here.

After four months, Amelia is running out of options to lift Michael's spirit. The Souhaugen gathered to discuss how they can help Michael. The group pitched in to clean Michael's apartment and pay some of his utility bills.

Then, Magdalena explained to the group that she has a friend from the University of Liverpool, where she used to study. Her friend at the university is doing a trial with volunteers who happen to recover from deep depression after 10 to 12 sessions with ayahuasca.

Ayahuasca is a psychoactive brew from two main ingredients. Firstly, the ayahuasca woody vine from South America which contains monoamine oxidase inhibitors (MAOIs). Secondly, chacruna (cotri veridus) leaves that contain the potent psychedelic compound DMT (dimethyltryptamine). Chacruna is sometimes substituted with chaliponga or chagropanga (diplopteryn cabrerana), which contains concentrations of DMT (5-MeO-DMT) in its leaves. Referred to by the Amazon natives as 'Yahe'. This gives a more intense visionary journey[9].

Amelia while in direct eye contact with Magdalena, nodding to express that she acknowledges where this conversation is heading: Ah, ayahuasca. I met a few people while I was in the Amazon who had experiences with it. It's served in a wooden bowl and apparently, it's so hideous to drink, that they wretch after smelling it. And after drinking it, they just carry on vomiting. That experience is supposed to be part of the cleansing process. The people I have talked to said that they had visionary of pretty pictures. Some had encounters with the higher world. Some had visions of monsters. Thanks for allowing us to consider this option, Magdalena. I will discuss it with Michael.

Amelia headed to drive to Michael's apartment. There he is on the balcony. Just staring blank to the horizon. He has grown a long beard that droops down along with his eyelids.

Magdalena: Michael, I'm about to discuss with you possibly the last option that could help you. If there is no progress from this, you are on your own. Only you can help yourself, you know.

Michael now showing a sign of being attentive: Ah, okay, go ahead.

Amelia: Magda discussed with me about a trial from her old university where volunteers are being lifted from their deep depression.

Michael: What do they have to do?

Amelia: The volunteers go into 10-12 sessions where they are given extended DMT which is directly fed in their bloodstream via a drip. The scientists allow the volunteers to be in peak DMT state for hours. The volunteers are put on MRI to monitor the brain. They are then debriefed about their experiences.

Michael: Which DMT?

Amelia: Think about it first before you decide. Ayahuasca.

Michael went to the kitchen while sighing. He pretends that he is looking for something. Amelia grabbed his hand and took him to stand in front of the bathroom mirror.

Amelia: Who do you see?

Michael: I see my young self, writing a letter to my Mom.

Amelia hugs him. Looking straight into Michael's eyes through the mirror: I see him too.

After a few minutes, they both sat down on the bed. Amelia gently took Michael's hand.

Amelia: It is not likely that you will be addicted to ayahuasca. I've done a lot of reading. Unlike LDS, nobody builds up tolerance to DMT. Ayahuasca hits the user the same each time. I also spoke with the organisers of the trial. They stated that volunteers are prohibited from speaking with one another before their debrief. However, after the trial, the volunteers then gather to exchange their experiences. Each of them shares the fact that they each encounter spirits from another world. But the amazing thing is that these spirits teach them moral lessons.

Michael straightened his back for once: Mom has not even come into my dreams.

Michael then nods to Amelia. No more words are needed.

A few days later, Chris rang Michael.

Michael: How the heck did you know that I'm going to the UK?

Chris: Don't do it, Mike. I beg you; it will just take you back to the fantasies in your brain.

Michael: Well Dad, you could be right for one. Or it could be that our brain is a receiver of consciousness that we still do not fully understand. Like a TV is a receiver of signals. Perhaps, the possibility of this kind of meditation is more important than our scientific selves.

Michael continued: Dad, before I let you go, I would suggest you read these two books. I'll give you a minute to grab a pen. Ready? Read the 'Discovery of Double Healing' by Francis Crick. He received a Nobel Peace Prize for his findings written in this book. The other is 'The Polymers Chain Reactions' by Kerry Mullis.

Chris: And then what?

Michael: It's up to you what you want to do. Just so you know, these two authors finished their books under the influence of psychedelics.

Michael then said: Have a good life Dad.

Michael blocked his dad's phone number.

It took two months for Magdalena to convince the trial organisers to allow Michael as a volunteer patient. Two of the current volunteers pulled out and Yoshi applied to go as a volunteer as well.

Jim the investor, funded Michael, Amelia and Yoshi's trip and stay in the UK.

Because Michael and Yoshi are prohibited to discuss their experience during the period of the trial and debriefing, Yoshi agreed to stay with one of the staff members at the University.

It's Michael's first session with ayahuasca. In just 3 hours, he is in peak DMT state. He is taken to the Amazon where his mother died. The last place he wanted to be. The vision is interchangeably seeing his mother's dead body to the time where Michael is crying as a boy waiting to see his mother again. Michael is overwhelmed with loss and grief.

Then, Michael is taken to the heart of the Amazon, over the canopy of Brazil nut trees and just below a light fog of clouds. His vision made him feel like he is laying on the canopy of trees while he watches the clouds become denser. Then, the clouds started to form some letters.

P R O P R I A A L M A.

Then more clouds spelt.

F E L I Z.

The formation of the clouds looked so pretty that Michael, for a moment, forgot about his grief. And he is smiling widely again.
As the clouds dissipate, two lights started to appear.

Michael: Hello, I'm Michael. Who are you two? Where is my Mom?

Michael looked intently at the female light thinking he has seen her before. She hugs Michael tight.

Michael: Alisa?
Alisa: This is Martin. He is one of our anchors. He will take us to Marima.
Alisa and Martin assisted Michael flying over the most beautiful spots of the Amazon. Though it was difficult to avoid bald areas of the jungle, some with smoke ablaze from the burning ground.

The three headed down to the next dense area. Alisa sees the Amazon River basin and they started to slow down. They landed beside Brazil nut trees which stands along the river. Michael is amazed at how tall the trees are. He estimated the trees to have an average of 49 meters high and their crown about 30 meters in diameter.

There, they found Marima guiding the agouti, rodents with chisel-like teeth. The rodents crack open the Brazil nuts. They followed her as she heads down the river.

Michael: Mom! Stop! Don't go to the river!
Alisa: It's okay, Michael. Marima is in spiritual realm, and nothing can harm her now. She could not complete her mission in physical form. Now, she is unstoppable in her world, which is parallel to yours.

Marima is too deep into her connection with the plants, trees and the agoutis that it took her awhile to feel Michael's presence.

Michael sighs with overwhelming relief to see his mother so peaceful and happy.

Michael: Mom, it's me.
Marima: Be happy with your own Soul, Son. Not to make me, your dad or anyone else happy. Your inner child led you here, he will continue to lead you. You do your best. Do not be afraid if you cannot complete all you mission in one lifetime, because our Soul will carry on and do the work.

After the 6th ayahuasca session, Amelia could see Michael's depression being lifted.

Amelia: It's so good to hear you laugh again, Michael!

After the 7th session, Michael's father rang him. Chris managed to get his alternate number. Michael told his father he would like no contact from him.

Michael: I will call you when I am ready.

During the last session, Marima led Michael to Western Amazon in Peru. From a distance, Michael sees a large tree house around the canopy. There sits Raul Stewart. An American adventurer, researcher and environmentalist. Raul is doing his own brainstorm in an A3 piece of paper.

He writes down a narrative from one of the loggers who said:

I will stop logging if someone would pay me to do another job. I love this forest, but I have a family to feed.

Raul draws a big arrow and writes in upper case letters: 'SOLUTION' inside a square. Turn loggers and miners to guardians of the forests. We will pay them better and offer them insurance too. Then he wrote, 'FUNDING', next step is to make contacts with influential people to help him fund his mission.
He then drew a large shape of a diamond. He thought, 'What am I calling this mission?" He paused for a few minutes just staring at the horizon.
'Ah, 'Forest Guardians'.
A few days later, Michael managed to contact Raul.

Raul: We cannot rely solely on the government. Commitment and funding are greatly needed for this heart-centred mission.

Michael: I agree. While we work on obtaining funding, we still need to keep a close network with the government.

When Michael is back in Australia, he continues to integrate and reintegrate his visionary experiences during his ayahuasca sessions to further heal himself.

Podcasters with high volume of up to 12 million subscribers in total have got hold of both Raul and Michael. During their interviews, both campaigned for funding.

Two years later, the Forest Guardians bought 2,000 hectares of forests and have employed 120 forest guardians.

Raul and Michael got hold of the son of a Brazilian politician. The son is 32 years old and became friends with Raul and Michael. The son, named Lucas, travelled to Peru to try ayahuasca.

A year later, Lucas was voted as the new president of Brazil. On his first month as president, he overturned the signed agreement for the build of 60 hydro dams in Brazil. He also combed the forest from illegal mining and logging.

While Martin has been guiding Michael and Raul, Alisa and Marima have been whispering to women all over the world. Explaining to them where gold comes from and how they are mined. Showing them through their dreams that there are sustainable alternatives to gold jewellery.

Chapter 35 – We Will Not Exist!

It's Yoshi's first session with ayahuasca at the University of Liverpool. His visionary experience took him to a cave, where cavemen drew images of half-human and half-fish. This session was short-lived. He got back to his accommodation and started to boil the jug to brew some Tokuyo Genmaicha. He didn't know what to make sense of his vision. Yoshi took out his journal and started writing. Nothing came to mind; he just wrote the date and location on top of the page. He stood by the kitchen bench and waited for 10 minutes. As he poured the tea in his tiny cup, he could smell the aroma of toasted brown rice from the tea blend. Then, a thought came. A word came to him which he has not heard before.

He quickly went back to his journal on the dining table and wrote *Inter-being*. He keeps writing; Humans, fish and the ocean need each other.

Second ayahuasca session. Yoshi feels the moisture of green grass under his feet. He is standing on someone's garden filled with different sizes and colours of hydrangeas. A mature woman opens a window and then she sat down in front of a wide and thick wooden study table covered with thick glass. Yoshi went in the house and watched the woman write with somewhat expensive pen. He walks slowly along the wall noting the woman's achievements over decades. It's Sylvia A Earle, writing her 2nd edition of 'Ocean – A Global Odyssey'. She noted on top of the page 'I must write this efficiently as facts can change again very quickly.' Yoshi noted her clear handwriting compared to his own in his journals. His session is again short-lived.

Yoshi bought Sylvia's book from a bookstore. It's very thick with beautiful pictures. He thought this is a lot to read. So, he also bought it from Audible and read the book with the audio. All Yoshi did for a week is go to his sessions and read and listen to the book which totalled to 14 hours and 21 minutes. Along the way, he took notes in his journal.

Third session: Yoshi sees himself laying on the bed during this session. He walks out to the nearby garden of the university. Fog started to come down and it got thicker and thicker until he could not see. A hand grabbed his arm. He resisted and tried to run. A woman with a long wavy hair told him "This way, Yoshi."
Yoshi: How did you know my name?
Woman: Hello, Yoshi. Lovely to see you again.
Yoshi: Alisa?
Alisa: This is Martin. He is one of our guides.
Martin: We appreciate what you have done so far with guarding our land through your plant-based cheeses. It's time to start the next step. We need you to safeguard our oceans.
Martin and Alisa flew Yoshi to the moon at night.
Yoshi: What has the moon got to do with saving our oceans. There's very little water here and they look like ice.
Alisa: Turn around, Yoshi.
Yoshi slowly turns to his right: Is that our Earth? Wow, it's mostly marble blue and white. I can see some brown bits, that must be Africa.
Martin: Yes, it is. We have taken you back to 7 December 1972.
Yoshi noticing some crew from Apollo 17 taking photographs of both the moon and Earth.

Before heading back to his accommodation, Yoshi bought some crayons and drew his vision of our Earth on the left page of his journal.

Fourth session: Yoshi heads to the moon again. This time without Alisa and Martin. He floats around the moon. He touches the crust. Yoshi feels the ominous atmosphere. He feels alone and sad. He turns and looks at our Earth. It's 2025. He noticed its colour is mostly pale blue. The white parts are a lot smaller. Yoshi could not wait to go back to Earth. He drew our Earth with colours on the right page of his journal, this time drawing with a lighter shade of blue.

Fifth, sixth and seventh sessions: Yoshi found himself floating around all the oceans. He watched industrial, commercial and illegal fishing. He watched parts of oceans go red. He watched many fishing workers get abused and get paid very little. He watched houses close to oceans and rivers get flooded. These sessions went for a long while. On the seventh session he wanted to wake up but couldn't. He found himself sitting on one corner of a fishing vessel, crying his eyes out as sea creatures are put back in the ocean, all dead. He felt so ashamed of being part Japanese.

Eighth session: Yoshi watched restaurants all around the world enjoying seafood. In the back of a restaurant, he slams boxes as he gets angry at how much of the seafood are wasted and thrown in the pile of rubbish. After the session, he wrote:

I understand that the Japanese turned to the sea as source of food after Hiroshima was bombed. There are so much more resources we can have now that induce minimum injury to our Earth. It is no longer necessary to overfeed ourselves. It is no longer 'after the war' when people were malnourished. Our eating habits need to evolve. If we don't, our Earth will turn grey, because the oceans are boiling.

Nineth session: Yoshi found himself floating around all of earth's oceans.
On the northeastern Atlantic Ocean, Yoshi is watching a small group of people at Long Island Sound which is along the coast of Connecticut and Westchester County. Long Island Sound is a small organic shellfish farm with diverse species of seaweed filtering out the pollutants, which then assist in reducing oxygen depletion and from these create a sustainable source of fertiliser and fish meal. [11]

Yoshi is watching from above. He could see the difference in the colour of the water within the vicinity of the farm. He noticed the temperature seem cooler. Clouds form around Yoshi and then he felt like he is being carried by two strong men. He was. Olav and Aleksander flew him across to the other side of the Atlantic. He landed in La Veta Palma in Southern Spain. [11]

The Elins did not say a word. Instead, they did a Japanese vow gesture toward Yoshi. Yoshi laughed and thought - *I don't even do that vow.*

La Vita Palma is a farm designed to restore its wetlands and while doing so, they created the largest bird sanctuary in Spain with over 220 species of birds. The birds flew all around Yoshi humming a beautiful tune of chirps. The birds started to poke Yoshi's shirt and pants. Then suddenly, the birds pulled and carried him over to the North Sea.

The birds slowly landed him on the lawns of Wageningen University in the Netherlands. There, he found, Roland Osinga. Yoshi watched Roland do his calculations that a when a network of sea-vegetable farms around the world, totalling 70,000 square miles, this could provide enough protein to everyone currently on Earth. It's even better because there are 10,000 edible plants in the Oceans. [11]

After Yoshi's session, he went to bed and wrote the farm details in his journal. He looked them up.

Yoshi: It was a dream. But these farms do exist! There is a lot of hope!

Tenth session: Yoshi's experience took him around the Pacific Ocean to see a woman named Kathryn Kroft-Ball. Kathryn is a Visionaire who believes in using technology to capture the 'dragons', the gaps and the exploration of the oceans[10].

Kathryn is presenting a webcast and explains:

People are empowered when they see what is happening in our oceans. They feel closer to the truth and do their best to find better solutions. The cameras expose entrepreneurs who are accountable to clean up any mess they make. Cameras and satellites also find where the most diverse spots are in our oceans.

Yoshi is looking at Kathryn's journal. He stares at one sentence - 'Ocean regulates the air.'

Yoshi is suddenly taken up high. He could see where the ocean deserts are expanding in the Pacific and Oceania. He breathes in the poor quality of air. Olav and Aleksander grabbed Yoshi form air and dove him down at 200 kms per hour, slamming down 500 feet below the surface of the ocean. There, the Elins handed him some kelp. A seaweed that can grow 9 to 13 feet vertically in just three months. Then, the Elins pointed out to Yoshi the kelp that are white and yellow, which are either dead or dying.

Yoshi looking confused: What do you want me to do?
Both the Elins whispered: Phytoplankton.
The Elins carried Yoshi to a few small-scale kelp farms in Japan, Taiwan, Tasmania, Australia and Stewart Island, New Zealand.

These farmers have figured out a sustainable way of growing kelp with seashells, particularly oysters because oysters filter nitrogen and mercury from the oceans[11]. These farmers have turned their farms as a source of food, feed for the animals, natural fertilizer and fibre. Since the farmers confirmed that seaweed composition is 50% oil, their farms have also become an important source of biofuels. The kelp, with the assistance of phytoplankton, grow faster than many trees and bamboos. These farms do not need fresh water; deforestation and it creates its own fertiliser[11].

Yoshi noticed that half the kelp seaweed is going white and yellow. Yoshi noted in his journal: Phytoplankton are microscopic marine algae, they are small, yet they produce half of the earth's oxygen. Phytoplankton have depleted due to the Earth's shift from Holocene to Anthropocene, where human domination, sucking the life out of Earth, have depleted nature's ability to sustain itself.

Yoshi highlighted in his journal to discuss Phytoplankton with Michael after the completion of their ayahuasca sessions.

Eleventh session: Yoshi watches progress being made in Mission Blue's Hope Spot in Madagascar. He admires the brave volunteers of 'Sea Shepherds' in Australia, filming fishing 'dragons' and actively cleaning up the ocean.

While in the Arctic Ocean: Yoshi watches Jacob and Bryan's friends, formerly from slaughterhouse and Mandara Oil Field. They found work in Newfoundland and Labrador, where the most abundance of fish is found. This is where 'overturning circulation' was first discovered. Where the key warm currents of the Gulf stream meet the upswelling cold nutrients rich water from the deep sea. A perfect condition for sea creature habitat. Jacob and Bryan's friends' job is to assist in expanding the area of overturning circulation.

Twelfth session is short yet very intense. Yoshi's future children and grandchildren appeared, and they stated: By 2050, if humans carry on the way they do, we will have more plastic in the ocean than fish. We refuse to be fed with food laden in microplastic, antibiotics, mercury and toxic chemicals.

Future children and grandchildren whispered to Yoshi: *The Oceans are the engine of our Earth. Without it, we will not survive. We will not exist!*

Yoshi woke up from his session and just unblinkingly stared at the ceiling. The staff member asked him if he is okay.

Yoshi: Yes, yes, thanks, I'm okay. I'm just bemused with my vision. Yoshi, of course could not tell the staff member what it is about. Yoshi is just quietly wondering to himself:

Hmmm, this is a test of faith. I have visions of my children and grandchildren, and I don't even have time to find a girlfriend.

Chapter 36 – Hands on Hearts Held High

200 people gathered at the Sydney Town Hall at 483 George Street. The Hall is buzzing with people's varying opinions. Lawyers, chefs, restauranteurs, angel investors, executives of nominee companies, wealthy mums and dads, nutritionists, specialists from the medical field, directors from hospitals and reporters from the media.

Members of the Soulhaugen register each attendee at the front desk. Each attendee is required to scan the QR code which requires them to enter their details, if they would like to invest and most importantly, they can enter a 52-character spill why they would like to invest. Each chair in the hall has a recycled piece of paper and pen.

The crowd settled. Yoshi waited a few seconds. It's completely silent. Yoshi closed his eyes and silently counted backwards, *5, 4, 3, 2, 1.* He started to speak calmly yet confidently:

Ladies and gentlemen, I welcome you to our gathering of action and active hope. The individuals who sit behind me are a part of a group who are giving their heart, sweat and soul for our Earth, so that our future children will exist. However, we cannot do it alone. We need each of you and we need each other. Those who care for our planet need funding and our collaboration will allow us to start and continue the work our hearts know we are here to do.

Lights at the Hall were suddenly turned off. The audible sound of waves started. The big screen started with a footage of Yoshi leading the camera crew to the kelp and seashell farms in Japan, Taiwan, Australia and New Zealand. Each footage showed how farmers are quite annoyed that the firm crew just turned up without permission. Yoshi managed to explain to them that they want to capture the reality of the farm. Yoshi explained to the farmers that they are there to promote for funding towards the farm. After a few minutes, the farmers are happy to be filmed and interviewed. All impromptu. No script. The farmers showed their authenticity about their mission. They truly care for our planet. However, they show some sadness in their eyes and their voices lowered as they sigh. They are struggling financially as they are unable to compete with the industrial sector. The screen turned off and the lights are turned on.

Yoshi started to ask the audience to grab the pen and piece of paper from their chair. He asked them to write the question:

How can we collaborate with our farmers so that we can continue to care for our planet? The audience is asked to just write down the question. An answer is not yet required.

Lights off. Big screen on. Satellites are shown from a distance, catching the patterns of the varying colours of the ocean. Firstly, showing the vibrant colours of where diverse marine life is thriving. These are in few small pockets. Then the satellites focused on the expanding desert ocean. Lastly, the satellite capturing the 'dragons of the ocean', leaving a big mess in the vast oceans.

Screen off, lights on. Kathryn Kroft-Ball is already standing where Yoshi was. Kathryn: We are grateful for the power of Telepresence. Write down this link and we can keep an eye and care for our Oceans at any time.

oceandiscoveryleague.org

The lights are kept on. Three young children walked from the right side of the stage. Two of them are the children of Sean and Ciara. The other child is the eldest child of Rebecca and Bryan.

The tallest child started speaking showing one of his drawings which is shown in the big screen:
This is the ocean full of plastic and nasty mercury. And this is the land close to where we live, and the trees are secretly being logged. When I grow up, where can I go? Can you please write down my question in your piece of paper? Maybe, our world is okay for mushrooms, but not someone like me to live in the future.

The middle child then started to speak quietly, showing her drawing of the ocean with lots of different colours of varied types of seaweed:

This is my dream. Rainbow colours of plants inside the ocean which we and all the animals can eat. But the plants in the ocean does not go away because they regrow themselves if we look after them. Can I ask you a question? Can you show me how I can make my dream come true?

The youngest child, a little girl, then started showing her very simple drawing of a page filled with waves and different sizes of fish. She said, “All these fishes hold air for us and all the animals”.

Two men from the audience stood up and started to walk towards the middle isle. One of the men saying, “Excuse us, we have to leave.”

The little girl asked. “But why?”

The other man nodding his head sideways and replied, “This is not going to make any money for us.”

The girl then said: “Well sir, try holding your breath while you count all your money.” [12]

The whole audience gave the children a loud applause and a standing ovation.

Once the children are seated with their parents. Lights off. Screen on. The footage showed La Veta Palma, Madagascar, and Hope Spots all around the world.

Yoshi started to read from his journal while the footage is being shown:

Good work has already started. Telepresence is easily accessible to all of us. Activism in front of major restaurants are showing footage of abuse of sea life and workers from industrial fishing. We can make incremental changes in our eating habits that can make a significant positive impact to our future. We ask you to collaborate with us to reforest our Oceans.

The footage continues to show multitrophic aquaculture farms with diverse species. Showing how these farms does not rely on antibiotics and fungicides.

Yoshi: Our farmers may be small-scale. However, many small farms dotted everywhere maybe the solution for our Oceans to regrow itself. Will you be the one to collaborate with us to make a decentralised system work?

Footage of plant-based boulangerie and patisserie and restaurants are shown dotted all over Europe.

Yoshi: In 2018, it was a challenge to find plant-based pastry in Paris. Now 'Land & Monkeys' and 'Wild & The Moon' are dotted everywhere. Michelin Star chef Alexis Gauthier is leading the way to 100% plant-based restaurants showcasing French and international cuisine, including a selection of plant-based sushi. Daimant Collective Paris is also gaining attention for their compassion to animals and their good food. Chefs are leading the way. They show all of us better food choices so that we induce the least injury to ourselves and our planet. Are you joining us? Because the oysters have! They are filtering the nitrogen and mercury from our Oceans!

The footage then shows children sitting in small groups of circles. They are drawing. The teachers have asked them to draw the dream place they want to have. The footage shows children from all six continents.

Yoshi: 16 is the magic number. 16% of the market share is what our planet requires to make our farmers become sustainable and to enable us to compete with the industrial and commercial world. We will start regardless, even if we start at 1%.

The footage then started to show children eagerly showing their drawings.

One of them said: This is me swimming. I have a big smile on my face there because I am no longer scared.

The cameramen asked: what are you scared of?

Child: Umm, the poison in the water. I don't want to swallow them. The child continues, and oh, this fish is also smiling because it's not swallowing poison anymore.

Yoshi: 2030 is the tipping point. Ladies and gentlemen, we have a short span of five years.

Yoshi asked the members of the Soulhaugen to stand beside him. Not knowing that both Alisa and Martin have been there all along. Alisa was the one who whispered to the little girl what to say to the men who left the Hall.

The Soulhaugen, one by one, cited their part of what Yoshi wrote in his journal:

A Promise

We are our ancestors' children.
They fought for our freedom.
We are ancestors to our unborn future.

A voice for our own and the many 7-year-old who suffer from unnecessary pain. Pain from imposed injuries through our food and environment systems.

Stress from imposed unrealistic expectations.

A promise to not just listen to their whispers.
Also, a promise to do the work.

This agency and courage, we have taken.
Like those who had the psychic dynamite who came before us.
Even though our ego makes us so terrified.
Our Soul knows we are meant to feel free.

Through their whispers and such promise,
To the oceans, we shall go,
We shall do and contribute love!

Then, there is complete silence.

Yoshi paused and stared at the audience. He silently counted backwards: *5, 4, 3, 2.1.*

Yoshi: Hands up those who are with us.

He suddenly became teary eyed. All 198 held up their hands high.

Chapter 37 – Brave

Bryan knocks on the metallic security door. It rattles. His mother opens the door, shaking slightly as she opens her arms to hug her son, Rebecca and their young son, Bene. They laughed out loud as they realised, they're all wearing a white t-shirt. Bryan's little sister, Lilly, run to the door and climbed behind Bryan for a quick piggyback.

Lunch is prepared on the long table in the backyard. Bryan rang Jacob so he could join them online. Jacob is ringing from Voyageurs National Park. He asked Bryan to call him back before bedtime.

Jacob: How are things in Albert Lea, Bryan?
Bryan: It hasn't progressed at all. It feels like there is less people here.
Jacob: That's expected. Do you remember the wolf I was telling you about? The one I saved here at the park?
Bryan: Yeah, the one that has the same name as Dad.
Jacob: Well, in the last few days, I 've been trying to get closer to him. And amazingly, last night, he just sat down next to me, and I slowly patted him. I was like, so enchanted.
Bryan: That sounds cool, bro.
Jacob: So, I talked to Dave for a while. And of course, he didn't say anything. We were just sitting along Ash River. I was surprised that I wasn't emotional at all. We're both seem carefree, you know. Just two creatures, hanging out. But just before I left to go to bed, he put his paw on my left foot. This is going to sound weird, but he looked intensely into my eyes and I then I get this vision. Now, bro, I want you to listen to this carefully, okay. I had this vision of Dad, at night, he was using a video recorder inside the slaughterhouse. He then opened the doors to let the pigs out. He was panicking as he picked up the little ones. I thought I saw him signalling to some people in big vans and pickup truck. He then used some wooden planks and used his lighter to set the planks on fire.

Jacob continues: My tears fell on Dave's fur and then, he run to the woods.
Bryan: Wow. Wow. All this time, we had no idea what he was really going through. Do you think he kept the video recorder somewhere?
Jacob: That's why I needed to talk to you. We need you to find it, Bryan.
Bryan: Of course. Mom and Lilly are in the middle of gathering their things to move to the new house. Let's just hope they haven't thrown it away.

Bryan spent two hours the next morning looking for the video. Lilly just woke up and asked Bryan what he is doing.

Lilly: Oh, I have it. It's inside my closet. I don't know how to turn it on, so I kept it safe here in the corner.

Bryan hugged Lilly quickly: Thank you, Lil' sis.

Bryan went to his room to watch the video and turned the audio off. Dave didn't just film that night. Some days, he secretly climbed up the metallic rails up to the chamber and on the ceiling. He quietly filmed when the sows are put in the farrowing crates a few weeks before they give birth. The film shows how small the crates are when the sows give birth and nurse the piglets, they end up squashing some of them to death. Dave filmed workers pick up baby pigs of which they think is not of good quality. They pick them up from their tails and smash their heads on the concrete floor. Dave secretly filmed on top of the gas chamber area where a few pigs are put in steel cages. The workers call the cages 'gondolas'. The cages are then lowered down where high concentrations of CO2 are released. Dave filmed the pigs intensely squeal, slam their bodies on the steel cages, gasping, their mouths frothing[13].

On a different day, Dave managed to discretely film a worker rape 'Bridget', a young pig. He captured how the managers and other workers ignored Bridget's screams.

Bryan turned off the video. He runs outside to try and release his traumas. He runs and run until he ended up at a lookout on a hill nearby.

He fell on his knees, he whispers: Dear God, please forgive me, how have I desensitised my emotions and guilt to these innocent creatures. They suffered their whole lives, so that we can have a few minutes of eating pleasure. And, and…Dad was suffering this, all that time, this…tug-of-war inside him. He was trying to be brave, but he gave in because he wanted to support his family. Oh my God, Dad, why didn't you ask for help?

Rocking himself while sitting down, Bryan reminded himself to exhale slowly. He then, did a two-way prayer:

Dear God, what would you have me do now? [14]

While Bryan was walking back to his old house, he had a vision of himself filming the current situation at the slaughterhouse.

The next night, Bryan and an old mate are dressed in dark overalls and balaclava. They dug under the slaughterhouse's fence. They are inside with their cameras. Bryan could not believe the stench that he was once used to. He filmed the areas where his father filmed. The two men left the slaughterhouse as if it's been left alone the whole night.

The next day, Bene run to the backyard as he hears his parents argue.

Bene: So that's what Grandpa Dave was like? He was very brave, but he was stuck in cognitive dissonance.

Bryan and Rebecca paused, and a sudden change of aura came over them, realising that they are raising a very intelligent child. Bene has been eve's dropping this whole time.

Bene: Can I watch both the film, Dad, please?
Rebecca: No, Bene, honey, it will be too much for you. You will have nightmares after watching them.
Bene: Well, I will let you know if I can't handle it, and you just turn it off. Mum, you said, for us to become great, we have to learn and face the truth, right?

Rebecca with hesitation still ringing in her voice: Okay, anak (child).

The family sat down and held each other just before Bryan turned it on. Bene and Bryan are crying the whole time. So was Rebecca while she tries to block the screen with her hands. She says: Dios ko, please forgive me, please forgive all of us.

As the second film finished, the family consoled each other.

Bene while crying: It's still the same! How can it go on like that! Mum, Dad, that is so unfair to the animals. My teacher said that it is scientifically proven a pig has the same feelings as a 3-year-old child. What can I do to stop that? How can adults build a place like a slaughterhouse?

Bene continues as he releases his emotions: It's like, like…HELL ON EARTH! Yes, us humans have created hell on earth, and they are everywhere. Mum, did you see how the pigs are doing their best to fight back? Did you see it? Did you see it, Dad? Can you please show me how I can fight back alongside them? They are not voiceless. Did you hear how loud they were screaming? But the workers chose to ignore their pain. We all ignore their screams and all their pain!

Bryan and Rebecca continue to hold Bene. Rebecca brushes her fingers on Bene's forehead, pushing his hair upwards.

Rebecca: We…we can start by not eating them anymore. Last Christmas was our last lechon (whole roast suckling pig).

Six months later, each member of the Soulhaugen group watch the documentary with the children. The doco includes most of the film clips from Dave and Bryan's recording. The film was watched far and wide. A group of Australians who live in London gathered and want to exercise their 'Right to know'. The group made a public request to the Australian government for an enquiry into the slaughterhouse practices.

Another six months passed, and the group's request have been blatantly ignored. The group then organised for the media to interview them and adamantly made their following arguments: [15]

We may think that animals are a source of food for us because they are weak and less intelligent than us. But it's only 132 years ago that we thought women were too weak and too dumb to vote. As Einstein said: "Everybody is a genius. But if we judge a fish by its ability to climb a tree, you will believe your whole life believing it is stupid."

A cow can smell, hear and sense pain and death from miles away. They can feel greater pain than humans can.

Animals cannot get out of the 'hell' we have created for them. Why don't we all spend at least a week in a slaughterhouse and then decide our food choices. Let us stop paying for animal cruelty ourselves. Let the Australian public know that the taxes they pay are contributing to this cruelty.

Watch the film and find out the hidden truths about where your food comes from. Enough of the lies about humane death. There is no such thing. Farmers can give animals a good life and then send them to slaughterhouse. No animal wants to be there and not one of them want to die.

This 'Hell on Earth' did not happen on its own. We create all of them.

A lawyer among the group insists: Laws on animal rights are already there. We just need to ask our leaders for the laws to be extended and asked them to be consistent across all types of animals.

We can no longer turn a blind eye and perceive meat as a symbol of status, power and source of protein. As more and more meat eaters are weakened by chronic diseases such as diabetes, heart and kidney disfunction. We are also becoming resistant to antibiotics as they are used in meat production.

Why did actor James Cromwell and director Chris Noonan become vegetarian and vegan as they produce the movie 'Babe'. They soon realised how intelligent the pig is.

During the media interview, a grandfather and his granddaughter told each other.

Each animal is a someone.
Bridget is a someone, who has feelings like your little girl or boy.
They are someone to - LET GO!
They are someone to - LOVE!

Many of the young generations in their 30s, 20s and as young as 11 years old watched the documentary around the world. The first flow on effect is the significant decrease in the demand for meat, starting in London.

The meat industry put forward a legal case against the filmmakers.

Marching in the main streets of major cities around the world, the animal protection activists resonate their messages with their somewhat timbered chants. Some members of the public just laughed, some threw whole apples from high rise apartments, some gave a respectful smile and a nod as they open their minds and hearts when they read and hear the activists' messages.

The film, the marches, the detailed raw footage that are free to watch from the website, led to public's awareness of the reality, the secrecy and deception of the meat, egg and poultry industry. External auditors ordered the government to do an unannounced investigation of the slaughterhouse all around the country, which led to a few being shut down permanently.

Chapter 38 – Freedom

It's 4.00am Sunday morning. In a deep forest of southern Queensland, Australia, footsteps make the crackling sound of dried leaves on the ground. A person is carrying something heavy. A few more individuals follow, carrying the same thing.

Bright orange Danaus Plexippus butterflies appear in hundreds. Then they hide among the Turpentine and Tallowwood and smooth barked apple trees.

The path is flat. The soil has a weak earthy smell. It smells more like ginseng root. The individuals lined up the heavy wooden chairs in front of a tall silver-leaved Ironbark tree. A group of the elderly sat down.

The Soulhaugen arrived along with a few of their family and friends. All standing on each side of the path.

Amelia arrived barefoot in a yellow long flowy dress. Her hair is gathered with a pile of Quandong seeds. The mild wind swaying the branches of the trees makes a sweet subtle whistling tune. Amelia is marched down the path by Rudy.

Michael is holding back his tears as he watched Amelia's beauty. His tears fell as he feels his mother's presence. A chair was left empty for her.

At sunrise, Amelia and Michael exchanged their vows.

Meanwhile, standing at 2,954 meters at the highest peak of Mount Apo in the Philippines, surrounded by cirrocumulus clouds, 120 Elins gathered. They are here to accept Alisa and Martin as one of them. The Elins gave both of them more power and insight towards an incremental protopian world.

When the Elins have gone, Alisa and Martin flew over to the 200-meter-wide crater with a small lake on top of Mount Apo. A stratus cloud formed, and a man started to appear.

They held each other and whispered, *I love you.*

In front of Father Joel, Alisa and Martin said their vows:

Our vow is for the Divine, our infinite higher force. A connection of love vastly pure and authentic like no other. Our love and connection with her are so deep it defines the very essence of our Souls' Freedom.

Three years later, Bene sits with his grandparents, parents and his two younger sisters. They sit along a table having lunch outside a garden near Lake Bito.

The adults discuss each other's progress.

Bene: Lolo (grandpa), on our way here, I noticed some trees with white leaves along the lake. Can we go there and see them?

Carlo: No, sorry Bene. I know the trees look beautiful, but I don't think it is safe there. Someone very close to your Aunt Alisa died there.

Bene: Did anyone else die or get injured there since then?

Carlo: No, I don't believe so.

After lunch, Bene sits on the grass between the tall papaya and a large wide mango tree. He closed his eyes, practiced his slow breathing, with the intention of erasing all learned fear he heard and felt today. He envisioned the white trees.

In their Airbnb, Bene went to bed early in the evening. He woke up at dawn and started walking. Because it is still dark, he got scared and started running. In 50 minutes, he arrived at Lake Bito where the white trees are. He rests his back against the trunk of one of them.

The tree shadows moved with the sunrise. Bene noticed that one area of the ground has unusual cracks. Bene started clearing the fallen branches and leaves. He could see something glossy between the cracks. He dug with his bare hands. He dug until his upper arms are full of dirt. He then used his legs and his feet to lift a sealed box.

He walked back. In his room, he quietly opened the box. Inside is a laptop, a microSDXC card and a small note.

A few years ago, Alisa had asked Father Joel to hide these for her. She was afraid that the mayor and his associates would confiscate them while she goes through the airport.

Bene inserted the microSDXC card.

There, he watched Auntie Alisa, dancing, flying freely.

References:

1. The Aborigines of Tasmania by H Ling Roth (Fellow of the Anthropological Institute), First Edition 1890, Halifax, England. F King & Sons, Printers and Publishers. Flinders Island of the Coast of Tasmania, English Words translation by Joseph Milligan (FLS) from Aboriginal words from tribes from Oyster Bay to Pittwater.

   The character of Thomas James is an inspiration and dramatization of the life of William Buckley. The Life and Adventures of William Buckley: Text Classics / Edited and introduced by Tim Flannery. Buckley, William 1780-1856, author. Melbourne Victoria: The Text Publishing Company, 2017.

2. Inspiration and dramatization from the life of David Alexander Good.
3. The Cheese Trap. Dr Neil D Barnard author. Grand Central Life & Style, 2017.
4. An inspiration and dramatization from the book: The Language of Trees. Katie Holten, 'Cacao – The World Tree and Her Planetary Mission' by Jonathan Miller Weisberger, pages 85-89).
5. The World in a Grain, The Story of Sand and How it Transformed Civilisation. Vince Beiser. Riverhead Books, 2018.
6. Inspired by and list from the Greenpeace Report (June 2022), 'Deep-Sea Disaster: Why Woodside's Burrup Hub project is too risky to proceed'.
7. The Language of Trees. Katie Holten, 'Joy is Such a Human Madness', The Duff Between Us by Ross Gay, p 223.
8. Inspiration from The Bob Brown Foundation.
9. Visionary, The Mysterious Origins of Human Consciousness (The Definitive Edition of Supernatural). Graham Hancock, Brilliance Audio, 2022.
10. Oceans: A Global Odyssey. Sylvia A Earle. Chapter 10 – 'The Future Ocean'. National Geographic Society, 2021.
11. Drawdown: The Most Comprehensive Plan Ever Proposed to Reverse Global Warming. Paul Hawken. Coming Attractions: Ocean Farming by Bren Smith, p 207-208. Penguin Books, 2017.
12. Inspired by quote from Guy McPhearson, scientist and professor at the University of Arizona.
13. Inspiration and facts from award-winning documentary film 'Dominion' and website by the Farm Transparency Project.
14. Inspiration from Letters from Love. Elizabeth Gilbert.
15. Inspiration from How to Argue with a Meat Eater (And Win Every Time). Ed Winters. Ebury Publishing, an imprint of Penguin Random House UK, 2023.

Your Notes:

www.ingramcontent.com/pod-product-compliance
Lightning Source LLC
Chambersburg PA
CBHW060612310726
48982CB00003B/534
* 9 7 8 0 6 4 5 5 8 0 4 1 9 *